Home
of the
Heart

MOUND CITY STORIES

Home
of the
Heart

MOUND CITY STORIES

Elizabeth Mills Irwin

TREEHOUSE PRESS
Littleriver, California
2000

© 1999 by Elizabeth Mills Irwin
First Edition, January 2000
Printed in Canada.
Published by Treehouse Press, an imprint of Earth Books
Post Office Box 494, Littleriver, CA 95456

Edited by Suzanne Byerley
Typeset by Jan Boyd
Book design by Elizabeth Petersen
Composition by Linda Richmond and Elizabeth Petersen

Photos of Methodist Church, Mound City Schoolhouse and Main
Street (page 77) reprinted by kind permission of the Mound City
Book History Committee. Harvest Scene photo (page 157)
reprinted from *Prairies* magazine © 1976.

ISBN 0-929151-07-0

Dedication

This book is dedicated to the most important people in my life: Horace, my joint tenant, who approved and endured; my children, Bill, Pat, and Nan, and Caitlin and Martha, all of whom insisted on this publication and helped make it possible; and my grandboys, Wayman and Santos, who were its inspiration. And to my mother and father who started it all, and my siblings Jack, Bob and Kathleen, who shared these adventures and of whom I took advantage in its writing.

Acknowledgments

༽

I acknowledge with affection and gratitude the help and guidance of my teacher/editor Suzanne Byerley, the computer goddess, Jan Boyd, Liz Petersen for putting it all together, and my writer friends who cheered, corrected, and lit my way through this process. Thank you, Meadow, Fauna, Lorel, Freda, Sunlight, Annette, Shanti, and everyone else who has listened and encouraged me, especially my friends at The Lodge at The Woods. I gratefully acknowledge chairman Lenore Pfeifle and the Mound City Book History Committee of 1984 and Allen Burke of the *Prairie Pioneer* for permission to use photographs from their publication.

Some of these stories have appeared in whole or in part in the *North Coast News*, *Mendocino Beacon*, and *Coast and Valley* magazine. Thank you, Jim Sears, Katherine Lee, Shelley Gerstein and Gale Mettey.

Foreword

This is an important year for me. My first book goes to press as I blow out the candles on my eightieth birthday cake. When you have been blessed with good luck, good health, good parents, a great family, as I have been, the advent of two grandsons who both celebrated their ninth birthdays with me this summer is sweet icing on the cake.

When my grandboys came into my life, I began to think more and more of the world in which I spent my early childhood, its pleasures, the freedom I enjoyed from fear and rejection, and the lessons that have stayed with me. Their world is a much bigger one, and a much more complicated one; I hope it will be as happy.

Because I know I can't be here for a lot of it, I want to help them to remember me. I want them to know a bit about where they came from, who came before them, and who their grandma is and why she is the old lady they know. I want them to know I love them with a love that I can't really explain or describe, a love that is special to each of them.

All of my eighty years I have looked back joyously on my Mound City years and the people who gave me so much. I remember them all with great affection. As I share these memories, I hope you, my readers, will share your own with your children and grandchildren.

Contents

Foreword 7

Home of the Heart 13

Who We Are 15

Broken Dreams 25

The Parsonage 29

Walking the Town 39

Monday Wash, Tuesday Iron 48

Merry Month of May 53

Company Dinner 59

Rain 64

Spring Cleaning 68

Sunshine's Season 72

The Whistling Jacket 85

Picnics at the River 89

Oh, Elizabeth 94

The Little Brown Church 99

A Garden's Secret 103

Lost at the Fair 106

Hot Day in Mound City 109

Flying with Aunt Sis 112

Visiting the City 117

Harvest Time 128

Autumn 132

Back to School 137

Keeping Up with Benny 145

October's Bright Days 148

Home Talent 151

November 162

Messengers 166

First Snow 168

Christmas Bells 171

New Year's Eve 175

Someone's Valentine 177

Losing Tonsils 181

Gilding the Lily 184

Turning Dead 188

Mother's Day and the Model T 201

Widow's Walk 209

The Last Day 213

Epilogue: Plain Art 218

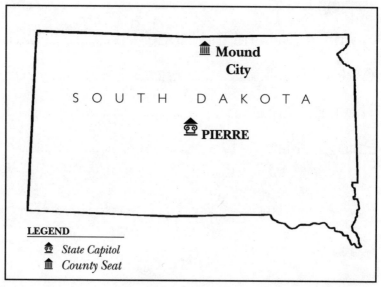

General map showing the location of Mound City.

Home of the Heart

⌒

FOR EVERYONE, at least for the lucky, there is a home, a
secret place to which one returns, in memory and in
dreams, for solace when today is a wrong day, when doubt
clouds the future, when wherever we are now, we need something that is not there. It is our heart's home.

In the dreams of many—and in the movies—this place
boasts wide lawns, white-painted gracious houses with broad
porches, dormer windows and cushioned seats, organdy
criss-cross curtains, polished wood floors and sweeping
staircases.

In my heart's home no elms arched across wide ave-
nues, no tumble of gold and flame colored leaves painted
the autumn scene. Mound City, South Dakota, stood raw,
almost treeless, in the unforgiving prairie. In winter our
brindle-colored, slab-sided house reared against the bitter
wind, homely with its skirt of manure and dirt my father
shoveled around it as protection from the cold. In summer
it burned in the brassy sun. There were no lawns and only

a few bushes nurtured and shielded against blizzard and drought. A very few twisted in the wind, froze and dried out in the open and survived. Hollyhocks were brave in summer, a background for the vegetable gardens. And here and there a patch of zinnias or bouncing bet defied the climate and persevered in soil cracked from lack of rain.

When my mind wanders back to that place, those days when mine was still the childhood of innocence, I hear the names of friends and neighbors who always welcomed me. I see them up on the stage in our home grown theatricals, I hear their voices in church and play with them at school and on long summer evenings. I remember the feeling of being a part of something bigger than I was, or even than my family was, but not too big, where there were no strangers and no enemies.

Even then, I knew I was very lucky to be me, one of the Mills girls, daughter of Minnie and Denny, of Mound City, South Dakota. I spent all of the first nine years I can remember there. I cried myself all the way to our new home in Pierre, where we moved in 1928. And Mound City has forever remained the home of my heart.

Who We Are

    ~

I THOUGHT OF MY FATHER as a very strong, imposing figure so it came as a great surprise when my grandmother told me they called him *Der Kleiner*, the little one, when he first came to their town. Their town was Artas, South Dakota, a community almost entirely of German immigrants and their families. That fresh little Irishman—Dennis Mills—from the city was a source of both amusement and scorn at first, and then dawning respect for his abilities as a teacher. But my maternal grandfather, himself an immigrant from Russia whose family had moved there from Germany, certainly didn't think he was a suitable husband for his daughter. These were not matters my mother liked to talk about. Although she didn't speak English until she went to school, she worked hard to lose any trace of accent and did not like to be reminded of her family's "old country" ways.

My dad loved to tell stories, so it was from him that I learned most about those very early years. In 1903, when he was seventeen and afraid of the prospect of a lifetime working in the underbellies of buildings in downtown Minneapolis with his father and his brothers, he ran away from home. His mother died when he was two or three years old and one sister, the only other child besides himself born in the United States, died when she was three. My Irish Catholic grandmother had followed her young husband from Ireland when as he said, he "tucked me Margaret under me arm and took a ride to England." He tucked several children too, but I'm not sure how many and there were more born in England; Liverpool, I think. Then Grandpa left his wife to care for the children and came to America to work until he could send for them all. Grandma Mills died when she was thirty-four, having given birth to thirteen children including three sets of twins. Only one twin, my Aunt Margaret, survived, but she lived a good long life. Aunt May, the oldest girl in the family, had to quit the fourth grade to stay home and keep house and care for the younger children.

My father's father had his faults—I remember him very little, he died when I was about five—but he tried hard to take care of his children and keep them off the streets. My father and my Uncle Jim told me stories of the boys they knew who had been killed in street disturbances, or ended up in prison. Grandpa was as hard drinking and as rough in his way as many of the other parents, but he set tasks for every child in the house every day, which had to be completed before he came home from work. They all knew he would not hesitate to enforce the rules he set. One that they laughed about when they were adults but which had humiliated them as kids was to be ordered to move all the coal from one side of the cellar to the other side in his absence. Another day he made them move it back again. It wasn't fun, but it kept them busy.

Both my grandfathers fancied themselves disciplinarians; their children saw them as terrors. Once my Aunt May Mills and another young girl who boarded with them, Mae Grace (who later married my Uncle Chris) got busy playing; they were after all, little girls. They forgot the bread they had set to rising and it was overflowing onto the table and down the legs when they heard the father footsteps returning from work. They panicked, pushed the bread dough back into the bowl and ran outside with it. Frantic, they decided to hide it in the outhouse until they could rescue it when he wasn't looking. But of course, Grandpa gave them no chance to get it. Much later he went to the outhouse and found it, risen and still rising, running over the seats and down the holes. They still shuddered when they told that story, but they laughed too, and he probably laughed a bit himself, after he meted out the punishments.

Dad followed a harvest crew through southern Minnesota into South Dakota. He knew nothing about farming, but he was a likable fellow, a great entertainer who could sing and tell Irish stories so they kept him on until the end of the season. He landed in Mound City with almost no money and no job with winter coming on. He overheard someone say they were giving the examination which certified teachers at the county clerk's office that day and he decided to apply.

He said the county clerk was teaching his dog to retrieve and all day during the examination, a newspaper would come sailing into the room where he sat and the clerk would bark, "Fetch." Dad said by the end of the day, the dog had become a retriever and he had become a teacher. Before the day was over he found himself on the back of a farm wagon heading into the country to the school he would teach and the farm where he would board. The driver of the wagon stopped at a cross road, pointed into the distance and said, "Zwei mile." Dad walked the two miles, found the farm house and began the career which he pursued much of his life.

He taught in country schools for several years, boarding with farmers, once sharing a room with the grandmother and the baby. He said first the grandma would go to bed, then Dad would enter the room in the darkness, averting his eyes, undress and slip on his nightshirt. Between the covers on his cot he would drift to sleep listening to the sound of the cradle being rocked. Grandma tied the cradle to her foot with a slender rope and at the first whimper of the child, rocked it a few times until there was quiet again. He said the sheets on the beds were home-made of black cotton cloth, so they would not show the soil That shocked my mother's housewifely soul.

Another place he boarded, he stayed home alone one Saturday when the family went to town. Usually he went too, combing the town for teaching materials, knocking on doors to ask for magazines, books, bright colored calendars and pictures, anything that would help him teach a room full of kids for whom English was a second language, or would be, as soon as they mastered it. But this day he was busy and enjoying the solitude. Once in awhile he heard strange scurrying noises from upstairs, but he found nothing amiss up there and finally decided there must be some varmints, rats or bats, up in the attic.

The noises continued and he began to imagine, he hoped, a strange sound, almost like someone moaning. Probably wind through the air vents, he thought, but finally decided to brave the attic and he was shocked to find a young woman lying on a bed, rhythmically wiping her head back and forth and making the weird noise. The "feeble-minded" they were called then, were often hidden from sight, felt to be a shameful thing that reflected badly on the family. This young woman was kept out of sight except for occasional times when the mother was alone in the house. She was given large doses of paregoric to keep her quiet and kept clean and well fed, but hidden from view.

At his first school, there was no clock, so he and the students ate lunch whenever they were hungry—sometimes ten o'clock in the morning, sometimes well into the afternoon if lessons were going particularly well. Sometimes he dismissed school early in the afternoon, sometimes forgot time and they went on reading until an irate father showed up looking for his kids. Everyone walked or rode a horse to school and the teacher was expected to get there early enough to build a fire and to keep the place clean, even the outhouse. But there were pleasant winter evenings when the parents brought supper and they had spelling bees, sing alongs, recitations and even plays.

Finally Dad got a teaching job in Artas and that's where he met my mother. She was Minnie Kusler, oldest of seven children of George and Mina Kusler and a teacher too, much to her father's dismay. Grandpa had refused to send his daughter away to Normal School when she graduated from the eighth grade. He saw no point in advanced education for anyone, certainly not a girl. Reading, writing and accounting, he thought, were plenty to make your way in the world. He was a buyer and seller of commodities, wheat, other grains, and cattle; he expected his boys to follow him and his daughters to marry prosperous farmers and do their duty. My mother was just as stubborn as he was and with the help and connivance of her Uncle Ernest, her mother's brother with whom she had emigrated from Germany and who owned a general store in a nearby town, Mother finally went off to Normal School for training in pedagogy, without help from Grandpa. She adored her Uncle Ernest until his dying day, and I fear resented her father until his.

So Mother and Dad got together, two teachers, she a pretty dark-haired, dark-eyed, stubborn first generation German American. He a stubborn, slight, handsome, black-haired, blue-eyed, first generation Irish American. I imagined him as romantic, fun-loving, witty, a charmer, but very serious about his work and a natural teacher. Mother was pretty, hard-working, intelligent, spirited, practical to her very bones, a talented seamstress and homemaker. Whatever my mother did, she did with a will, with great expenditure of energy. In fact, I don't think she ever just *did* anything, she tackled things, hard. Every chore—cleaning, cooking, washing and ironing—was accompanied by a flurry and clatter.

How I wish I knew more about that courtship and those very early years before I came along and before I can remember anything. Mother and Dad were married in August, 1915, and my sister was born a year later. Grandpa Kusler hadn't spoken to them since their wedding day. Either the first signs of the stomach cancer which eventually killed him or the birth of their first child made my grandfather forgive my mother for marrying a feckless Irishman, a schoolteacher without an acre to his name, no money and few prospects as far as Grandpa could see. Despite his disapproval he had probably been secretly amused by Denny when he boarded in the Kusler home for a time and had with Mother's brothers kept the house alive with practical jokes and music. Once he shaped pillows in my Uncle August's bed, drew a face on a pillow slip and used a mop for hair. When the delinquent son came tiptoeing to bed in the wee hours, trying not to wake his father, he started to slip between the covers in the dark, and dimly saw the apparition. A woman in his bed! He let out a startled yell and Grandpa came roaring up the stairs.

I'm sure Mother was happy her new husband had a job in Mound City, almost thirty miles away from Artas, so that she need not live under her father's disapproving eyes. She would miss her mother whom she loved and who was the peacemaker in that house, keeping at least some kind of lid on the volatile, tempery father, and would miss her high-spirited brothers and much younger little sister, my Aunt Lisette. My uncles Albert, Ernest, August and Edwin, veterans of World War I, I remember as handsome young men who laughed a lot when they weren't around their father. The other brother, Calvin, stayed away from home after the war and died as a very young man. I knew him only from stories and pictures of him, his beautiful wife and baby son.

These early years were complicated. First my parents left Mound City when my father took a job in Wallace, a town some miles away, and there they survived the flu epidemic of 1918. They were part of a brigade of well people who fed and nursed the sick and dying. When my mother realized she was pregnant and too far from the beloved doctor who had delivered my sister, she reluctantly gave in to coaxing and agreed to go to Minneapolis to stay with Dad's family and have her second baby, me, in a hospital. Her face got grim whenever she spoke of that experience. She was forced to lie in bed laboring, was not allowed to walk around to relieve the pain, was not even allowed to have anyone else with her. I was the only one of her four children she did not have at home. Fortunately by the time my brothers came along, the family was back in Mound City and Dr. Volleben was in charge. Rumors persisted about the good doctor, that he had been trained in Vienna, that the scar on his face was from a sword blow in a duel, that he had been a noted doctor until his problems with drink drove him abroad. However he came to us, we were grateful for his presence.

My parents' marriage must have had its rocky times, but I was oblivious of them then. My father was the leader, the dreamer and the planner. My mother made things work. Dad worked hard and turned his small pay over to her. She had a way with money. She could stretch it, spend it so sparingly and so wisely, I don't think we ever looked poor even when we were at our lowest ebb. Dad was known to chafe sometimes under her tight control and do something foolish. More than once he was persuaded to buy some "heirloom" from a poor down and outer who, Dad said, "just needed a hand." Mother was usually hard put to swallow her rage at this misplaced kindness. She was a firm believer that charity began at home, or ought to.

Still, I remember my mother breaking into a smile, her whole face lighting up whenever my father came into view. She cheerfully, mostly, picked up after him, ironed his shirts just-so, turned his collars just-so, and cooked for everyone he invited home to dinner, even on washday. With no thought of the problems it might cause the little woman, Dad tended to extend these invitations lavishly to anyone he ran into—a book salesman, a farmer buying feed, Dr. Volleben in town to make house calls—the prospects were endless. He was always directing a play or some kind of home talent show and time after time, Mother wistfully watched our front room furniture, even the curtains, being carted off to decorate the stage. But she was always proud when people applauded loudly and told her what a gem Denny was.

My sister, Kathleen May, had what I considered the never to be overcome advantage of being the first born. Blonde and blue-eyed, she was pretty as a peach and the apple of everyone's eyes. Bright and neat, she loved nice clothes and clean ones. She hated being dirty. I gather it gave her some pause when a second child was born when she was three. Innocent but just retribution, I suppose, that she couldn't pronounce Elizabeth correctly and for some time, despite my parents' earnest coaching, called me Libashit.

Our relationship had its bumps when we were very young. To have a messy, demanding, loud-mouthed invader disrupt your three-year-old reign as queen was a trial to her. And I always felt like a tag-along, less competent, thoughtless, more than a bit on the scruffy side. I hated the comparison but I really didn't mind a little dirt, my shoes tended to be untied, my sashes dangled and my hair was often straggly. Kathleen insisted on starting to school when she was five because her friends were a year older and they were going. Our parents decided to let her go, sure she would give up and drop out in a day or two. But she didn't and that meant she went through all of her school life being at least a year younger than everyone else in her grade. Personally I welcomed her departure every day, it meant I was number one around the house for those hours.

Of course those pesky boys, my brothers, showed up— Jack in 1922 when I was just three. His real name was John Charles and he was a thoughtful child, his big gray eyes studied the world around him. He was never giggly unless he was being tickled which reduced him to complete helplessness, but occasionally he would reward someone in his little world with a rare shy smile. Kathleen and I were quite willing to make fools of ourselves to make that happen; it took us some time to learn that wasn't the secret. In fact I don't think we know the secret to this day. It is still his.

Jack always went about his business quietly, leaving our parents to discover what they could when they could. When he was a tiny boy, about three, while Mother was busy with the baby, he toddled down the gravel road to Noste's store and started to pull away the red wagon he had spied while there with Mother a day or two before. Mr. Noste asked him how he was going to pay for it and just grinned and accepted his answer when Jack said, "Charge it." Of course he got to keep the wagon and sometime later he carefully painted it with a pail of syrup Mother left behind when she pulled the groceries home in it.

Brother Robert Louis—Bob—came along two years after Jack. He was usually a sunny little boy but he had a very hot temper. When my Aunt Sis came out from Minneapolis to live with us and Mother took a job in Dad's office, Aunt Sis insisted she couldn't do a thing with him, and I can see him to this day, his little diapered bottom hunkered down in the dirt, saying, "No." He had dark curly hair, big brown eyes and was cuddly. He talked early and we could never be sure what he would say. No secret was safe. He staggered along, clad only in a diaper, hanging on to our dog, Buster.

Buster, a big white and gold long-haired collie kind of mutt was the boys' constant companion. Bob learned to walk hanging on to him and used him as a pillow for his naps. He was Jack's shadow and protector on his first solo forays into the big outdoors. We all loved Buster and he lived with us happily for many years.

And we all lived together in a little crooked house— well, not quite crooked, but probably not the house of any person's dreams, at least not any sensible person. I thought it was perfect.

Broken Dreams

I REMEMBER WHEN WE MOVED to the parsonage. I must have been three, for Jack was born in an earlier house, one that was much too small for a family with three children.

I remember the echoing empty rooms with their raw wood floors. And the stairs that led to the upper story, so narrow you felt squeezed, and so steep every climbing was an adventure for a little girl. My father shooed me ahead of him up those stairs and into two giant (I thought) very empty rooms only partially divided from one another. "This is where you'll sleep, Elizabeth, and Kathleen too." It seemed a very large and lonely space and I was only partly comforted by the knowledge that my big sister, she would have been six, would be with me—in the same bed. We didn't have that many

Downstairs again, I saw my mother on her hands and knees in the kitchen. That shouldn't have been too surprising for it was the way my mother "gave the floor a good scrubbing every week," insisting that we kids stay outside or in the other room until the linoleum had had a chance to dry. But this was different. She held in her hands a funny little yellow odd shaped cardboard box—it was not very fat and had what looked like a beak on one end. And she inched along the wall squeezing the little bellows along the top and bottom of the molding that covered the joint between calcimined plaster walls and wide board floor topped with an ugly green and brown linoleum. I'm not sure I thought it was ugly then, but in retrospect I know it was.

"What's that?"

"That's so the bedbugs don't get you."

"Do we got bedbugs?"

"Maybe. But we won't have when I get through."

Mother turned back to her labors and I wandered around the rest of the house. Bedbugs were a common concern. In those days of little water that took enormous amounts of energy to pump and bring in for cleaning, laundry, cooking and bathing, women battled bedbugs the way city people now battle cockroaches. Constantly.

My mother was a clean woman. She never finished her efforts to overcome dirt and grime and bedbugs. And mice. Every fall, with the first nips of cold weather, the field mice found their way into our house looking for a warm, dry place to build their nests and for table crumbs and whatever diet a careless housewife's pantry might provide. My mother was not careless and she kept an eagle eye out for any damage her offspring might do. Still now and then we were plagued by mice and Mother was tireless in her efforts to get rid of "the darn things." That was as close as she ever came to swearing. But she was a demon with the mouse traps despite her aversion to killing. She held the full trap at arms length and carried the limp little bodies outside somewhere each morning until she was sure the species had learned its lesson for the season.

I don't remember anything about the actual move, but somehow the furniture was carried in, beds made, dishes put away and the pantry shelves lined with jars of home canned goods and bags of dry foods like flour and sugar, and pails of syrup and peanut butter and lard. And I remember finally sleeping in the big empty room upstairs in the bed with my comfortable and comforting sister next to me. It seemed to me that first night I would never sleep again. I lay staring in the dark trying to remember what I would see if I tiptoed over to the window. Koch's house across the road, I liked that thought. And my mother and father down in the supposed-to-be dining room in their bed. I lay very still hoping I might hear them breathe. Jack, the baby, was with them. A hired girl was coming to stay with us. She would sleep on the other side of this wall.

If I got up and looked out the window of the room where she would sleep, I would see the pump and the coal shed. I lay there trying to remember exactly where everything in my familiar world was in relation to this new house. The leather duofold and armchair I could picture in the living room. The round table was in the middle of the kitchen and the wooden cupboard stained dark hung where my father had nailed it to the wall nearest the dining room.

That cupboard held almost everything that was precious to my mother. There were cut glass bowls and dessert plates and glasses. There were hand-painted china plates and tea cups and the company dishes. There was a handsome pitcher and heavy glass candlesticks and "the darling teapot." Whoever had given it to them had called it that and it was the way I always thought of it. These things had been my parents' wedding presents and my mother cherished every one of them. With a few hand-embroidered table linens they lifted her above the meanness of our ugly brown house, and reminded her that there was a world of beautiful things that still might be hers someday.

One night some weeks later, a rogue wind blew up from the north, a cold, vicious wind that penetrated the thin shell of our house and whistled around the chimney. I fell asleep burrowed deep under the covers so that I wouldn't feel it or hear it and curled into as small a ball as was possible so the wind couldn't find me.

When I woke it was still dark but my sister had already left our bed. I could hear voices, and something else, a terrible sound. Moaning, keening—a mourning sound that my father's low rumbling voice couldn't seem to stop, couldn't comfort. Barefoot, I ran down the cold stairs and peeked my head out the door into the kitchen.

My mother was sitting on the floor, her body hunched and her hands wringing. Her hair was hanging around her face and I couldn't see her eyes. My dad was looking sick and my sister sat on a kitchen chair so quiet it was like she wasn't there. The baby was fussing in the next room.

Mother reached out and touched the pile of glass and bits of china around her. I couldn't see the cupboard, my father must have leaned it against the wall. He bent down and picked up half of a painted tea cup, handle intact.

"We could glue this, Minnie. It would still look pretty."

"Oh-h-h-h , no," she cried and reached out to brush the damage aside. She stumbled to her feet, pulled her hair back, wiped her nose and started rattling pans at the stove.

When we were summoned to breakfast, the cupboard had disappeared and the kitchen was neat in the icy morning sunshine. But my mother looked different for a long time. I missed her smile.

The Parsonage

P ERCHED ABOVE THE DRAINAGE DITCH that ran beside the graveled road, our house was the Methodist parsonage, which we were allowed to rent because the congregation could not afford a regular preacher. It was just a collection of boards and shingles with some doors and windows, though not many of either, and next to the Methodist church it reared against the prairie sky, an ugly monolith, brown, awkward, untrimmed. There was no softness in its outline, no curves, no porches or trellises to break its bleakness. Much as I loved it, for it was home, I dreamed someday of a bay window with a cushioned seat where I could sit and read and dream and of a generous white columned porch that would embrace the house and invite me into its shadows on a hot day. It didn't occur to me that these graces would adorn some other building. I simply saw them transforming this house, my house, into something more beautiful. More beautiful, because I accepted it as beautiful in its present state. And I knew it smelled good.

Smells were important to me. I was conscious of how different other people's houses smelled, not necessarily unpleasantly, just different, strange. Our house smelled like my daddy's coffee and cigarettes and the sauerkraut and sausage my mother cooked for us. It smelled of the bread she baked, of bacon frying and a hot iron on starched clothes. I loved the smell when Mother would plunk the iron freshly heated on the coal stove down on a limp, wrinkled white rag and turn it into a shiny white shirt releasing a starchy, Sunday kind of smell. Our house smelled of us, a family of six trying to keep clean with the water we could pump in the back yard and carry and heat for washing and baths and laundry. I thought it was a pleasant odor of warm, busy people who worried and talked and laughed and told stories and quarreled and made up.

The floors of the house creaked and the narrow wooden stairs that led to the unfinished upstairs were steep and always dusty, no matter how often Mother swept them. The front room was brown—brown walls, brown leather duofold so it could double as a guest room, matching rocker, and heavy wood picture frames with dark paintings. One was of an old sea captain at the helm of his ship. Another large one that hung near the front door, I learned later was called Christ in the Temple, but for years I thought it was a picture of my mother in a white dress pointing to two loaves of freshly baked bread in response to my father's usual question, "What's for dinner?"

The dining room turned into my parents' bedroom whenever a hired girl came to live with us but when we were on our own, we used the embroidered tablecloth and the company china and ate there when we had company. I remember once my little brother picking up his plate on one of these occasions and asking to my mother's embarrassment whether she had borrowed the dishes from Mrs. Koch, our neighbor. "They don't belongs to us," he said.

Very young Bob always said whatever he was thinking, but we thought he was so cute, nobody minded much. Once when Aunt Sis came from Minneapolis to visit, we were riding in the car, she in the front seat with Dad. She turned to say something to Mother sitting in back with the four of us, the small boy studied her gravely for a minute and then piped, "Aunt Sis, you is cwooked." And so she was, or looked at least, for one canine tooth grew longer and farther out than the other.

One night as we all sat at the big round table in the kitchen, homework finished, our cups of goodnight cocoa drunk, my father read us the last poem of the evening. Each verse began with the words "Be glad," and listed the simple everyday things that were reasons for light hearts and gladness. Poem over, Mother marshaled small Bobby, wearing only a diaper and shirt, black curly hair standing about his face, to the narrow stairs that led to our beds above. He began his climb on all fours until about three steps up, he turned and stood a tipsy moment facing us and said, "Daddy, is you glad of me?" My father laughed and wept and hugged the small boy, and I, unable to handle so much frank emotion gracefully, or jealous of the attention, promptly leaned so far back in my chair that it tipped over and banged against the wall. I cried, Bob was carried off to bed, probably a few sharp words were spoken although I don't remember them, and the day was finally over.

The kitchen was the center of our house. The big black coal range kept it cozy in winter and there Mother cooked and baked, heated water for baths and laundry, and kept the "sadirons" hot when she ironed. The big old round table surrounded by six unmatched chairs in the center of the room was where we ate and studied, it was Mother's work space when she rolled out pie crust or kneaded bread dough. With two dishpans, one for washing and one for rinsing, Mother washed and Kathleen and I wiped the dishes. Here friends and neighbors sat to sip their coffee and visit or play whist occasionally on a Saturday night and my friends and I gathered for bread and jelly treats or to play school on a sleety afternoon. Sometimes at night we would play Uncle Wiggly, a board game, or color and draw and cut out paper dolls and their clothes. Most of their clothes came from the Sears or Montgomery Ward catalogues which we learned to cut out leaving flaps to turn down so they would stay on the doll.

A washstand stood next to the door that led to the "shed" and then outside and held an enameled wash basin. The slop pail sat beside the washstand. Inglorious and apt to be smelly if not diligently cleaned every day, this vessel was the repository for potato peelings, dishwater, all of the usual kitchen garbage. Any household that had chickens threw this mixture out to feed them. We had chickens once. But my father did so hate the mess they made in the yard and even worse the job of killing one for Sunday dinner that he prevailed upon Mother to go back to buying them from Mac the butcher, or some farmer friend who would deliver a chicken all cleaned and disemboweled along with a couple of dozen eggs and a quart of whipping cream on Saturday when he and his family came to town.

The only other piece of kitchen furniture was called a safe; it had a narrow galvanized zinc shelf and room to store flour and sugar. Unfortunately, the kitchen walls were so interrupted by doors, one to the dining room, one to the front room, one to the pantry and one to the shed, there was very little space left for furniture. The pantry stored jars of jelly and jam and vegetables and sauce Mother canned each summer and all of the staple supplies except those that were stored in the fruit cellar/cyclone cellar where we kept potatoes and apples and carrots and other winter vegetables. On one wall of the pantry a window had an opening which could be closed by a wooden flap, and here Dad attached a cold box where some foods could be kept cold, probably frozen, much of the winter.

The back door was the only door that enjoyed much use, and you entered the house through a narrow shed with hooks on the wall and low benches on either side. Here we hung our coats and caps and woolen mufflers and stuffed our overshoes underneath the benches. In summer there was a washbasin and an extra pail of water so we could wash our hands and feet before entering the kitchen. In winter we sat here to pull on the stubborn, awkward overshoes that were mandatory once snow fell. We were usually in too great a hurry to buckle them and went about clinking in the cold air. Occasionally, for I tended to be awkward, I would get the buckles of my two overshoes caught together and fall ingloriously in the midst of a run for home or school. I fell so often, tripping over myself, that I almost always had scabby knees and ankles, unlovely sights that worried my father and offended his sense of aesthetics.

At the top of the narrow stairs, the walls were bare wood, and there were no closets except for hooks screwed into the walls and curtains that Mother hung to make an enclosed space. Sometimes our parents' bed was in the first room at the top of the stairs and under it Mother hid fruit cakes and Christmas cookies in long cardboard boxes or wooden apple crates carefully covered in newspapers and old towels. That room also served as hallway to the other one where two double beds took care of the sleeping needs of my sister and me and my two brothers. When Martha, our hired girl, came to live with us, she shared the bed with me and my sister gratefully moved into a cot of her own. The stove pipe from the front room coal stove ran through the upstairs and provided the only heat for the two rooms only partially divided by a wall that did not go all the way to the ceiling. Here we could lie and watch Jack Frost's tracery on the window and when we felt brave, face the cold and jump out of bed to write our names in the thick frost. Bare of insulation or even plaster, the place was freezing cold in winter and burning hot in summer.

In winter we would drag our clothes under the quilts and dress in the tent they made, aware of the goosebumps on our arms and legs and not unpleasantly aware of our own and each other's smells. Then we would rush downstairs to hug the front room stove while we buttoned and laced and got ourselves tidily together. In summer I liked to lie abed amidst the early morning clatter and watch a spider building a web in the corner and the dust motes float between floor and ceiling and smell the smell of raw, bare wood warming in the summer heat. As the day wore on those rooms upstairs grew unbearably hot, but what a treat it was to emerge from bed and put bare feet on sunwarmed floors instead of the icy ones of winter.

Behind our house was the coal shed which held not only coal but the tubs we used to carry it in on the red wagon and a few cast-offs that had not yet been recycled. Very little was wasted in our society, someone almost always had a use for another's discards. When one wonderful day we got our first car, a brand new Model T, the coal had to move over and make room for that black beauty.

Between our house and the Methodist Church there was an old wooden piano box in which I loved to curl up

and read on a piece of abandoned carpet. One day someone, probably a student of Dad's, put a badger he had
caught in that box and forever after it had the smell of the
fear and rage of a wild thing captured. I didn't enjoy reading there anymore.

There was also a funny peaked shed, narrow and high,
which someone years before had painted an acid green but
which had so faded in the sun and rain and snow that it
only had remnants of the color where the wood had sliv-
ered away. Here we played a favorite game called "Aunty-I-
Over." And in the unmowed prairie grass which constituted
our yard, we caught grasshoppers and held them before
our faces insisting they spit tobacco, and chased each other
with our rubber guns—rudely carved wooden guns with
strips of inner tubes stretched their length. A direct hit stung
a bit and our calls of "Bulls-eye" and "You're dead" signaled
our triumphs. And here in winter we built slides of
mounded snow over which we would pour cans of water so
the whole thing froze into a glistening ice raceway. Down
we careened, bodies, sleds, cardboard, our noses running,
our cheeks red, chapped, bringing on a fresh crop of chilblains which would sting and ache all night.

Of course, we all had privies behind our houses. They
tended to be a bit smelly in summer and freezing cold in
winter. In all seasons, they were very hard on the delicate
behinds of little children. Ours was a two holer, both holes
of equal size so little people had to brace themselves with
both arms to avoid sinking too far for whatever comfort
the place afforded. I never heard of anyone actually slipping through, down, down into the terrible known, but I
could imagine it.

Some privies were fancier than others. Ours was an
unpainted little shed with an almost flat roof and one high

window with screen but no glass. We had an ordinary cut out about three or four inches square in the door that was originally also covered with screen but when that fell out or rusted away, I don't recall that it was replaced. After all, kids let the door stand open much of the day so that little screen offered no protection against flies and mosquitoes.

Other people had privies painted to match their houses with a glass window, set high, of course, to shield the user from view, and fancy cut out designs in the door. Stars and moons were popular. A humorous book about all of the fancy ways people tried to decorate their outhouses was written by a man named Chic Sales, and that is what privies came to be called, the Chic Sales. Some people tried lining the seats around the holes with sheepskin or some other soft material to make it a bit easier on the behind parts and to cut down on the danger of freezing. It would have been nice I am sure, but Mother thought with a house full of kids, lined seats would be hard to keep clean and might be an invitation to loiter. Loitering was discouraged.

But on a warm summer day it was not unheard of to sit quietly for quite awhile, overalls dangling around one's feet, listening to the lazy buzzing of flies, dreaming a little, resting from picking potato bugs or a hard game of King of the Hill or Pom Pom Pull Away. Sometimes there was enough of the catalogue left to be of interest—two button shoes or three, red checked gingham or blue could be quiet considerations. If you were sharing the premises with a friend it seemed to bring on confidences and long conversations about school, parents, siblings, books we were reading.

There was always a box, usually an apple crate, which housed the "toilet paper," often the crinkly harsh wrappers that apples came in, or oranges if anyone could afford them. Or the catalogues—we called them "Monkey Wards" and

"Sears and Sawbuck"—and we only had to use the thin pages, without colored pictures. They were the softest.

The outhouse was a very democratic place and there were few issues of age, even of gender, if the concerned parties were young enough. If Mother caught my sister or me heading in that direction, she was wont to insist we take a little brother with us. That was all right except it meant unbuttoning and lifting and wiping and then buttoning again. And if it was cold we didn't want to stay out any longer than necessary. If it was warm, there were always important people waiting or a game left unfinished, and I tried to avoid taking care of Jack or Bob. But Mother had an instinct or an eagle eye, or both, and oftener than not I got caught.

Keeping the privy clean was a big job. Mother slopped Lysol around and Dad shoveled lime down the holes to reduce the odor and resist the flies. When a privy reached a certain degree of fullness, another hole was dug and the building was moved. The old site was filled with dirt and ashes and in no time the grass grew over the site. Those holes were the repositories of discarded glass and tin cans and decades later became the source for antique bottles and other treasures.

When my youngest brother was a baby my father installed a chemical toilet upstairs and my mother made flowered curtains to surround it for privacy. It was a big tank, partly full of a strong disinfectant and with a real toilet seat and cover. Its use was discouraged; you had to be sick almost unto death to be allowed to use it, especially in nice weather. Unless it was freezing cold, I actually preferred the outhouse—I didn't think it smelled any worse.

The other emergency equipment was a china pot with a cover under every bed for night use. Women made crocheted covers for the lids, hushers they were called, which kept them from clattering when the pots were in use. It was getting up in the night to carefully squat over that pot and not tip it that made me first aware of the big advantage boys had with their equipment. I began to believe that boys, males of all ages, had the best of things.

On a miserably cold day, icy wind, sleet, snow, how wonderful it was to see our old brown house against the prairie sky promising warmth and food and my mother's presence. On a hot one, the washtubs full of water sat warming in the sun near the pump and we played in them by the hour, my brothers and I, in just our underpants, browning until we became the color of the hazelnuts we found in our Christmas stockings. In every season, it was home.

Walking the Town

⌒

THE HIGHWAY RAN THROUGH THE TOWN like a graveled ribbon. It was our Main Street and in the middle of town
it was partnered by a splintery wooden sidewalk which
turned left (west) at the Mercantile and ran up the road
past the post office and almost to the Methodist Church
and our house, the parsonage. My parents kept the church
clean and rang the bell on Sundays and on Christmas and
New Years Eve promptly at twelve midnight.

Just beyond us, the road petered out at a rutty lane
that crossed it and ran along the Noste property. If you
followed that lane north, it would lead you to the schoolhouse and to Larsen's pasture. To get to Larsen's house
you had to cross a cattle guard, an arrangement of pipes
over a drainage ditch, set just far enough apart to discour-
age the cows from crossing. It discouraged me too, but I
crossed, gingerly setting first one foot and then the other
on the slim pipes, nursing the painful pleasure of fear. I
could imagine my foot slipping and hear the crack of my

ankle bone as it broke. But Sonny Larsen was my friend, sometimes my best friend, so of course I couldn't stay away from his house.

When you entered town from the south and if you turned left, the first road you crossed would take you out into the country to the Heislers and the Knudsens. On the other side of Main Street that road took you to "The Grove" officially Vroman's Grove. Mr. Vroman gave it to the town for family picnics and a place for kids to play. It was the only oasis of shade during the dry sunburned days of summer. There were almost no trees in Mound City then and little decorative greenery of any kind except what grew naturally and survived the worst of summer. Our water came from wells in our back yards and just to keep enough pumped and carried for regular household use and the requisite vegetable patch was all most of us could manage.

My sister and I walked the road, past the grove every day to fetch milk from the farmers who kept cows, syrup pails precariously balanced, one in each hand. Those pails got heavy and to our mother's chagrin, we were known to set them down and stop to pass the time of day and maybe kick a few rocks with the Kightlinger kids while the milk soured in the sun.

Heading north on through town toward Deibert's Hill, you passed a crossroad on the left which would take you up past Hans Anderson's house that was behind ours or to the Lutheran Church if you turned right. At the top of Deibert's gentle hill you could just get a glimpse of their pond where we sailed our washtubs and boilers, ahoying and avasting, ye lubbers. Sweat poured from under our eye patches, down our dusty cheeks. Often we were distracted from our game by water snakes, scooters and dragon flies, all of which defied my efforts at capture.

I thought Mound City was a pretty town. Most of the buildings were painted white with green trim, except for the brindle brown of the Methodist church and our house, one tannish yellow and one light green one that I seem to remember and Hans Anderson's was gray, as were the Lutheran Church and parsonage. I realize now the town was dusty, bare, and almost treeless with only a few hardy shrubs here and there that could survive without watering.

Every passing vehicle on Main Street flung dust on porches and through windows. The slightest breeze, not to mention the ubiquitous prairie wind, raised dust and deposited grit on carpets and in eyes. Housewives equipped with only brooms, mops and carpet beaters fought valiantly. They shook the dust from their line-dried laundry and scrubbed the kids, at least where it showed, in all but the coldest weather under the backyard pump.

There was more than one way to walk home from school and choosing which route to take required considerations of time, season, and the chances of getting caught loitering around town in my school clothes. My mother knew well that unless I headed straight home, looking neither to left nor right and never stopping to scale a fence or jump a ditch, stockings would develop holes in the knees, black bloomers would lose their elastic and the hem of my dress would inevitably come loose.

Poor Mother, no matter how sternly, how often she cautioned, instructed me to "be more careful," even scolded, night after night she sat in the kitchen under the kerosene lamp mending and patching the garments of her second born.

In the fall, the first frost turned the Russian olives dark and plump and sweet, never mind the residual puckeriness. We walked home each school afternoon down the lane to the Noste's tree. There we stood leaning against the wire fence feasting on the small, sweet, plump fruit which we had been testing for weeks. Day after day we chewed the mealy little berries, risking terminal pucker, until just the right kiss of frost followed by sun turned them into our autumn treat.

The trouble with walking home past the Russian olive tree was that it inevitably led past home and Mother and that meant stopping to change clothes. And maybe no way to get free again for the last precious hours of daylight. I might get asked to help out with "the boys," or reminded to bring in the coal or to polish the lamp chimneys. That meant I wouldn't get to walk downtown or stop to visit Mr. Finkbeiner at the blacksmith shop.

The first time I heard the poem about "Under the spreading chestnut tree, the village smithy stands," I knew they were talking about Mr. Finkbeiner. I had never seen a chestnut tree and he clanged and pounded wagon wheels and tended his forge fire in a dark earth-floored building with a door wide enough to let wagons roll through. But as the poem described, he was a mighty man, with powerful sinewy arms and strong black hands. Winter or summer, I could stand for hours inside the doorway, safe from flying sparks, and watch him work and sweat, drops running down his face into his thick black mustache.

I thought the world of Mr. Finkbeiner. He never stopped his work; I don't think he ever touched me, but he would flash his strong white teeth in a wide smile and call a greeting. I knew I was welcome for as long as I wanted to stay. The mingled smells of hot metal, cool earth, horse droppings and urine, and the rich sweat of my hero were perfume.

When I could tear myself away, I would head for the courthouse. Even after my father's office as county superintendent of schools was moved to its unlikely location in the jail next door, I enjoyed visiting the courthouse. I thought of all the people who worked there as my friends. There was Chester Solmonson and Mr. Hegel and Judge Kruger. They all had time for a word, a smile, sometimes a handshake or a pat on the head. Chester was the handsomest man in the whole world and the Judge awed me with his solemn dignity and formal greeting.

Everyone knew who I was, the farmers transacting business in the county offices, the clerks, sheepish trespassers of the law waiting for a turn in the judge's chambers or courtroom. I felt perfectly at home and no one ever questioned my presence or ordered me to quit the premises. Sometimes a peppermint or an apple, soft from a warm pocket or sunny window sill, was pressed into my hand. Often people asked after my mother and sister and "how are those little brothers?" they would say.

I lingered, smelling the spittoons and the dry wood of benches, wainscot and trim and watched and listened to the conversations around me. The courthouse was always a little dusty and dry-smelling, but it was a friendly haven from hot sun or cold wind.

Finally, I headed for Dad's office, threading my way through the jail and stopping to chat with the occasional prisoner and the sheriff, Johnny Solmonson. My father's office was a not too neat nest of books and papers that smelled of his cigarettes, furniture oil, sweeping compound and him. Sometimes I could curl up in the extra chair and read one of the books that came to him from publishers and book salesmen. Sometime he would be busy, talking to a discontented farmer who wanted to keep his kids out of school and in the fields or who objected to something in the course of study.

Readin', 'ritin', and 'rithmetic were enough for any farm kid, some of them felt. Extras like poetry and literature and art appreciation or geography beyond the boundaries of South Dakota, maybe even Campbell County, were frills which cost too much money and took too much time away from chores. When these confrontations were in progress, Dad would wink at me and lift an eyebrow and I would slip away. Usually he could charm the complainer, get him laughing over a good joke or two, compliment him on his fields, his kids, his wife's homemade pickles and send him back to the country shaking his head over the funny stories and resigned to his kids' continued schooling. My father liked these hard-working farmers, respected them and envied their prosperity and they could feel that.

On down the main street I would stick my head in at the bank and wave at Mr. Larsen and anyone else who would notice me. It was always cool and a little dark in the bank and I liked to look at the inkwells built into the counters and watch the dust motes dance in the sunshine that penetrated the dim interior.

Sometimes at this point I realized I had skipped Koch's garage and retraced my steps to get a good whiff of gasoline and make a few tracks in the oil on the floor. Mr. Koch, we always called him just plain Koch, would favor me with a smile and pretend to reach out to pat me with his greasy black hands. When I drew back in mock terror we both laughed and I went back past the bank to the meat market.

Mac the butcher might have a message from my mother for me to bring home some wieners or round steak or to stop at Noste's store or the Mercantile for something she didn't have in her pantry, canned or dried, or in the fruit cellar, protected from heat and cold. Mother knew my route and could always catch me somewhere along the way. Sometimes Mac would give me a wiener or a slice of bologna and I would stand around chewing, inhaling the smells of fresh meat, old blood and sawdust, and listening to his foolery, joshing me or anyone else who came in the shop. Then I would say good-bye and cross the street.

The hotel seemed like a grand building to me. It welcomed me as warmly and took my presence as much for granted as any of the other establishments I visited. I loved to peek into the dining room and watch the ample Mr. and Mrs. Johnny Solmonson taking a breather sitting at a table nursing thick white mugs of coffee. I could smell the delicious kitchen smells of fresh bread and steaming soup, exchange a few words, wriggle in pleased embarrassment at a kind joke or two at my untroubled expense and continue on my way.

Noste's store smelled the best of any place in town. Richly combined, the odors of floor oil, kerosene, dill pickles, sauerkraut, peanut butter, syrup, spices, candy and the warm bodies of undeodorized people delighted my senses. Mr. Noste loved his jokes and I knew when I entered the store, he would be ready for me. One year his arms and hands were covered with the ugly sores and scales of poison ivy and he kept threatening to hug me and pet my face. I was repulsed by the angry eruptions but he giggled so hard, I knew he would never cause me any real harm or humiliation.

He would stand behind the counter wearing his black sleeve garters and sleeve protectors. "What can I sell you?" he'd say. I'd shake my head. "Nothing? How can I get rich if you don't buy anything? Come on, maybe some candy or a pickle? How about some sauerkraut?" Then he'd whip a bag of groceries off the shelf and push it into my arms. "Hurry up now, mama's waiting."

The "Noste boys," Tupin, real name Arthur, and Olaf, joined in friendly good-byes and I headed off toward home and supper. The post office and the Mercantile would have to wait for another day. There was only time for a quick visit with my friends the Kolodzie boys at their parents' combined pool hall and candy store and a bit farther up the road toward home, with my best friend Pauline. I learned early just how far I could push my mother and when I had been commanded to bring home supper groceries was no time to loiter.

I never got enough of my little home town, never got tired of making my rounds, never doubted the cordiality of my welcome, never wearied of its smells. If I timed it right I might share an afternoon snack at the telephone office with the Falde kids. At the Mercantile I could wander through the displays of yard goods and overalls (which we called overhalls) and sniff the Johannes Brot, an evil smelling pod carefully dried and sold for its curative powers. The Alexanders, Joe and Ada, seemed to like me and I envied their daughter Martha Jane. I thought she was the luckiest little girl alive, indulged just as I would have liked to be. With a handful of cheese and crackers or gingersnaps, she held court in front of the store in nice weather and inside among the dry goods when it was cold.

Finally home, Mother took her groceries, shook her head at me and ordered me to wash and set the table. My sister was busily helping and the two boys were under everyone's feet. In a minute or two, Dad would poke his head around the door calling a greeting to all of us and asking, "What's for supper?"

In winter we ate by lamplight, in summer by the fading light of a long day. My sister and I still had homework, perhaps coal to bring in, lamp chimneys to wash and dry, and there were always the dishes. Late into the evening Mother would be busy setting bread to rise, clothes to soak, ironing to be sprinkled, mending—always busy keeping us fed and clean. By eight o'clock I was tired enough to troop out to the outhouse "one last time" with the boys and off to bed. Kathleen was allowed a later bedtime. I was often too sleepy to argue.

Every day was a good day for me, full of adventures, playmates, adult friendships. There was so much to do, so many wonderful places to be and people to be with, although I could not stay awake another minute, I couldn't wait for morning. Lucky was the child who lived in Mound City.

Monday Wash, Tuesday Iron

~

MONDAY WAS WASH DAY. You could count on that; it was an immutable fact that nothing could alter. I think my mother thought it was the eleventh commandment. Snow, sleet, hail, rain, somebody's birthday, a funeral, you still got the wash out bright and early Monday morning.

A line of clean clothes dancing in the prairie wind was evidence of good character and high moral standing. "She puts out a nice wash" was a compliment that made a newcomer's entry into society a much surer thing than it might have been. Not that everyone lived up to the standard set by a few women like my mother, but those who didn't had to have a good many other likable traits and it took them longer to be accepted. A new bride who met the challenge was judged likely to have a head start on matrimonial success.

At our house, wash day actually started Sunday evening. No matter what the social plans for the day, picnics, potlucks, an evening of whist, everything came to a halt early so Mother could get started on the wash. "Wash day, my eye," my father used to say, "it's a season." He hated it and none of us enjoyed it but Mother had the satisfaction of knowing she had done the right thing at the right time and done it well.

As soon as supper was over and the four kids were settled at something, out came the piles of laundry to be sorted according to color and use. Bed linens in one pile, towels and washcloths in another, underwear, stockings and color fast cotton garments in yet another. The wash tubs and boilers, when they weren't in use on this day or for Saturday night baths, hung outside on the north side of the house. They had to be assembled in the kitchen and pail after pail after pail of water had to be pumped and lugged into the house. Certain white clothes like my father's white shirts and the sheets were boiled to get them clean and white enough to dazzle the most critical eye. The rest of the things were soaked overnight. By bedtime the whole house smelled of Fels Naptha soap that my mother whittled into a pan of water and cooked into jelly.

Monday morning long before we kids were rousted from our beds, my parents had set up the old cradle type wooden washing machine next to the house, carried the tubs back outside, kept the wash boiler steaming away to provide hot water and begun the laborious process of washing, wringing, rinsing, wringing again and hanging to dry. Dad's main job was to rock the washer while Mother turned the wringer and finally pinned the clothes to the line. He gulped a cup of coffee and hurried off to work when the last load had been washed leaving Mother to finish and put away the tubs and dispose of the dirty water.

In winter the clothes froze on the line and Mother brought them in to hang on temporary lines strung about the kitchen to thaw and finish drying, her hands beet red and cracked from the cold. On rainy Mondays the same lines festooned the whole house and Dad had to struggle the heavy washing machine into the kitchen to do the job. Wind was always a problem on the prairie but especially in March clothes had to be anchored with double the usual number of clothespins.

Noon dinner was a hastily put together snack of left over potatoes fried in bacon drippings, a few slices of grayish cold roast beef, some warmed up canned peas perhaps and a jar of peach sauce from the pantry. And supper did not promise to be much better for Mother would be worn out with the day's labors. If we were lucky there would be a big bowl of German slaw, plenty of bread and butter and more of the ever present home canned sauce. We all looked forward to Tuesdays.

One August morning when I was about six, I was standing with my mother holding the bag of clothespins and handing them to her as she pinned the clothes to the line. The sun was already shining hot and bright and the clothes gave off that wonderful aroma of sun warmed freshness that made me enjoy working beside her. The morning was peaceful, my nine year old sister was in charge of the two little boys, all of the town's women were busy with their own washing so the telephone was quiet. I was looking forward to a long lazy day as soon as the clothes were all hung. Mother handed me three washcloths and told me I could hang them my very own self but "get them nice and straight now, Lizabeth," she reminded.

Some weeks before, the man who owned the lot next door, I don't remember who he was, had come in and plowed it all up. I thought the freshly turned dirt would make an interesting change as a play ground, Mother hoped he planned a nice garden, although she wondered where the water would come from. And when nothing happened as time went on we forgot about it and paid very little attention as the earth dried and turned to dust in the summer sun.

Right after noon dinner that day my mother eyed the sky questioningly. There were some big thunderheads forming off to the northeast. "Everything is pretty dry, girls, let's get it in before a storm hits," she called, instructing the boys to "sit right there" on the back steps. Scooping up the clothes basket she ran for the clotheslines and Kathleen and I followed. By the time I was wrestling with the second clothes pin on the washrags I had hung up, the wind hit, screeching out of the sky, whipping the clothes around the line.

"Girls, get the boys inside," Mother shouted and we headed for the house, hardly able to breathe for the dust that came whirling in from next door. Through the window we could see her struggling with the clothes, chasing the basket across the yard, and finally giving up when pelting hail stones made it too painful to stay.

The storm didn't last long but the damage was done. Everything left on the line was torn and twisted and dirty. Wearily Mother began the task of hand washing the shirts and dresses. Sheets and towels we shook vigorously, my sister holding two sides and I the other two but they continued to smell dusty the whole next week when we slept in them or dried with them. When my father came home, it was to find the house festooned with washing, the sleeve of his favorite white shirt damaged, beyond repair he thought, and no supper started. He and Mother walked outdoors to kick at the piles of hailstones melting in the reemerged sunshine and check the garden which looked as if it had been trampled by giants.

We were all subdued the rest of the evening but Mother rallied to make bacon and egg sandwiches and she sat that night under the flare of the Coleman lamp carefully mending Dad's shirt in preparation for Tuesday's ironing.

Ironing days were better. Mother started a pot of her succulent stew or a huge pan of macaroni and cheese which she could keep an eye on while she worked. The kitchen smelled of starch and good food and I liked playing with my doll or coloring at the big table while Mother ironed. I was jealous when my sister was allowed to iron dresser scarves and even her own dress, she was careful and adept at such things. But finally it was my turn and I cheerfully ironed the dish towels and my own handkerchiefs.

When my father came home for dinner at noon, the ironing board was pushed aside, a nice hot meal was set on the table and he brought the cheerful news that since the storm had been mercifully short, the garden seemed to be struggling back. With luck we would still have some beans and peas and the lettuce would surely come through again.

Dinner over and the dishes done, Dad went back to work, Mother allowed herself a little nap with the boys and I was free to spend the long bright afternoon at anything I desired. Time was forever, I thought then, I would go find my friend Pauline and together we would walk all the way to The Grove with our dolls, and play away the long afternoon, two busy housewives and mothers, exclaiming over the dangers we had survived the day before, chatting busily in the shade of the cottonwood trees.

Merry Month of May

～

SPRING HOVERED OVER THE PRAIRIE the whole month of April, but it hadn't yet come to stay. One minute the sun was warm on our faces and we shed our coats and caps half way to school. Minutes later it seemed, clouds sailed in on the prairie wind and we shivered with cold.

My sister and I both hated the offending winter underwear that our mother insisted upon until she was sure the season had truly changed. It was thick and itchy with long sleeves and legs that had to be wrapped and tucked beneath our black stockings in the hope they wouldn't show. My sister came close to that objective but no matter how carefully I folded and worked, holding my breath to ease my black stockings over the darn things, panting and almost weeping in frustration, eventually I gave up and let the lumps show.

One warm spring morning, we stopped on our way to school, shared a knowing glance, ducked into the coal shed and like a couple of snakes shed our outer skins of bulky

53

woolens, slipped off the offending undergarments, one piece, button down the front with a drop seat, and hurriedly hid them under the coal tubs that hung on the wall. On our way home we would change our clothes again, redon the longies and bring in the coal without a reminder. Our virtue would be rewarded, no one would be the wiser and we would be free as two birds for the day.

But of course, Mother did know best and that afternoon a late snowstorm moved in and she decided she couldn't wait for our after school coal delivery and went to the coal shed to get some. We had been too hurried in our efforts and a telltale leg of one pair of underwear hung down below the tub for all to see. Aha, the miscreants were caught. She filled her pail, left the evidence in view and went back to wait for us. Talk about the spider and the fly. We waltzed in after school, a bit more disheveled than usual perhaps, it had not been easy in the sudden cold to disrobe and dress again, but innocent in everything but deed. Mother thanked us for the coal, commented upon the unseasonable weather, looked carefully at our throats and hoped out loud that we wouldn't be taken ill.

"Funny thing, it was so cold I had to go out for coal this afternoon."

Oh oh, she knows! But that was all that was said and we relaxed. When bedtime came, Mother came up to tuck us in and say good night and she picked up the offending garments.

"Hmm, these smell like coal dust, can't imagine why, and look, at the black streaks."

We broke down and told, of course, on ourselves and each other, and mourned the passing of that strategy for feeling and looking in step with the season. From now on, we'd have to wear the hateful things until Mother decreed long underwear days were over until the next winter.

May was welcome. Rare, although not unheard of, were snowstorms in May. The pastures were green, the cottonwoods in The Grove and the boxelder tree on our road were leafing out. The maypole had first appeared in the playground some weeks before the great day of celebration, May 1, May Day. There it sat, towering gracelessly in the mud and snow waiting for a day when we could practice dancing. We called it dancing. Holding on to strips of colored cloth, make-believe at this stage, we were supposed to weave gracefully in and out, crossing and recrossing our ribbons. If we were successful we would end up with thick plaits of many colors which were finally wound around the pole, unwound and wound again, all to the piping sounds of the school Victrola playing a song about the "merry, merry month of May."

Unfortunately, the weather seldom allowed the attachment to the pole of real ribbons, actually strips of cloth dyed in pastel colors, until almost the day of execution. I choose that word advisedly. But finally close to the fateful day, there we were, galumphing around in our muddy overshoes trying to remember over, under, over, under. The teacher called out instructions, first in joyous exhortation, finally plaintively pleading. I, for one, forever mistook my overs for unders, confused my lefts and rights and headed off in the wrong direction at the outset.

"Now over and under. Elizabeth, you are going over not under, no, no, now under, now over, under, over."

Hopelessly out of step, my friends and I would fall into heaps of collapsed laughter, but by the day of the performance, we summoned all our dignity and danced a sprightly step around the maypole. When we got confused our parents suppressed their titters as best they could, applauded appreciatively and brought out the lemonade and cookies. Only the poor teacher and those little girls who were adept at overs and unders and lefts and rights, were upset. And their mothers no doubt regretted the long lamp-lit hours sewing the white dresses and preparing the flower crowns that were our costumes. I'm sure my mother held her breath, hoped for the best and prayed her second child would outgrow her clumsiness.

The moment school was over we dashed home to get on with the most important celebration of the day—May baskets. Evening after evening we worked on baskets of woven paper strips, tin cans and oatmeal boxes covered with crepe paper or adorned with tag ends of doilies and tissue paper. Now the day was here and we scoured the pastures for mayflowers, pasque flowers officially, and any other early blooms we could find. Sometimes we happened on a brave bluebell or a johnny-jump-up and we picked the tender shoots of green grass to line them. Hastily we filled our baskets, adding a cookie or a piece of home-made fudge, and waited impatiently for first dusk.

The early dark was filled with flitting figures, boys and girls, hurrying from house to house scattered throughout the little town. A quick hard knock alerted that a basket had been delivered and we hastened away to hide and watch the reaction of the recipient. The fancier the basket, the more heavily laden with goodies, the more affectionate the message and the more important the size of the smile.

Before school was dismissed for summer vacation there was one more big event. We called it Rally Day and the children of the country schools and other small towns gathered on our playground where broad jumping pits and a pole vaulting structure had been prepared. Here after months of practice, we vied with one another in one hundred yard dashes, relay races, potato sack races, broad jumps and high jumps. Only the older boys were allowed to try the pole vault. It was important to bring our school a suitable number of ribbons, blue preferably, but red or white were better than none, so we had practiced religiously and we tried mightily. When I won the broad jump and had a place on a winning relay team for eight year olds, I was as proud as any Olympic gold medal winner. After the games we feasted together and sang songs and our teacher saw to it that we neither bragged unfittingly nor lapsed into depression over our losses.

At last school was over and we hurried out into the sunshine, intoxicated with our freedom, torn between running home to share our excitement with our mothers and dallying along the way together, reluctant to part and close this special day.

"No more pencils, no more books, nor more teachers' cross eyed looks"—we tossed our papers into the air and laughed giddily. Of course, we, at least I, picked up those papers, for my father countenanced no littering and would have been frostily disapproving if any effort with my name had been found blowing in the wind.

When my own children began to bring home their school-made tokens of love for Mother's Day, I tried hard to remember how we had marked that day in my very young life. I have no memory of coloring a card or imprinting my palm on a specially painted cardboard plaque. I don't think I ever wrote my mother a love poem or painted for her a self portrait. I wonder why, perhaps the day had not caught on yet in our part of the world.

May was a special month and it ended as it began with a celebration. On almost its last day we trooped to the cemetery to honor our dead. The grass had been mowed and many people had been there earlier to clean the graves and trim the scraggly bushes. On this day we brought wreaths and flowers for everyone and American flags to honor those who had fought in war, War Between the States or the Civil war, the Spanish American War and the Great War, World War I, which many of us were convinced had truly been the war to end all wars. Some of us wore angel costumes with gauzy wings, and together we all sang and prayed and people wept over their dead. There were flowers for every grave, and headstones were carefully cleaned of winter dirt so the names could be read aloud. There were tears over the dear departed and comforting pats and croons and then we all repaired to The Grove and brought out the fried chicken and potato salad, one woman's coconut cake, another's devils food, until the tables groaned and we paused to eat. Kids gave up their romps in the sparse grass, men broke the little knots of conversation that had entertained them and the women wiped their flushed faces with a dish towel and sat down to enjoy the food. I was almost giddy with relief for although I did not have a family member in this cemetery, the cloud of grief that had hung over the gathering had made me want to cry. May had come to an end, a full month bursting with excitement, happy and sad, and I could think of June.

Now we had the long lazy days of summer before us; I was free to wander the town and the countryside in my favorite old play clothes, held hostage only by the chores that I was expected to share. There were lamp chimneys to clean each day, potato bugs to pick and drop into a can of kerosene, but there were also long hours to explore, to hunt for garter snakes and trap gophers and to practice swimming at Hesler's Dam, which we cheerfully shared with the cows.

Company Dinner

M Y MOTHER WAS HAPPY. She got her dining room back and she wanted to celebrate. When my Aunt Sis came to live with us she took over the second room upstairs that my parents had slept in. And so my parents slept in the dining room. But now, Martha, our hired girl, was a member of the family, comfortable enough with all of us to not mind sleeping with me in one of the double beds, the last baby was old enough to sleep in another with his older brother. My sister Kathleen could queen it in a bed all by herself—she loved that, and Mother and Dad could have their space back.

Personally I was quite happy to share my bed with Martha. I liked her a lot and she was a big healthy girl with solid haunches and wide shoulders. On a cold winter night she was a great comfort.

Mother had invited company for dinner, Chester Solmonson and his beautiful wife, Lily. He met Lily in New York when he was in the service in World War I and because he was a handsome, charming guy—a black Norwegian, I understood—he eventually won her hand, as my story books often said, and brought her to Mound City to live. It was a worry to most of Chester's friends who fell in love with Lily instantly, that she could be happy in a little prairie town with none of the comfort and excitement she knew in New York. If she was unhappy with us, she never said so, but we all thought of her as fragile and someone so precious we tiptoed around her.

Personally, I thought Chester ought to be enough for anyone. I was completely in love with him, his huge brown eyes, his shiny black hair and full curved lips. I was willing to be his slave, so if looking after Lily pleased him, it pleased me. I must have driven her crazy hanging around her, so close I would be the very first to know if she needed anything. Or perhaps she might grow faint, I almost hoped so, and press the back of her hand to her forehead the way heroines in books did and I could run and fetch her the smelling salts—whatever they were.

Mother fussed over that dinner, she wanted everything to be just so. Her cheeks grew redder by the minute and her eyes gleamed more brightly as she checked the oven and tasted and tested. Finally she lined us all up and with my sister's help, scrubbed our faces and hands, ears and necks and elbows, "check their knees," she enjoined my sister. And then dressed in our best, our Sunday School clothes and it was only Friday, she sent us off to the front room to sit quietly, and she did mean quietly she said.

Martha had cleaned the house before she left to go home to the farm. She liked us, but she missed her big family of sisters and brothers and went home for frequent weekends. Before she left she had helped Mother set out and wash the company china and glassware. The white on

white embroidered tablecloth with lacy cut-work was ready
and so were the matching napkins.

Dad blew in from work and crowded the kitchen with
his presence. He had to wash and shave at the washstand
and he couldn't resist peeking into the pots and pans and
opening the oven. He inspected the apple pies waiting in
the pantry, and then decided what the table needed was a
centerpiece. My mother blanched. Dad's centerpieces were
not always as successful as might be hoped. We didn't have
an easy supply of flowers, even in summer, having to carry
water precluded that. But Dad was ingenious.

Sometimes he was satisfied with a vase full of interesting grasses, we had a lot of those growing in patches here
and there. Sometimes he used vegetables from the garden.
But this time he was reduced to cutting fronds of tum-
bleweeds and although they were pretty enough, he said,
they were too colorless to show up at the table. Right there,
in the midst of Mother's frantic preparations, he plopped
down at the kitchen table, her only work surface, with a
glass of water, a set of paints, some brushes and a pile of
thistles. He experimented with colors and brushes until he
produced a really quite handsome cluster of painted thistles
which he put in the black vase someone had given them as
a wedding present. Mother, who had been trying desperately to hold herself in check, sighed with relief, shooed
him off to join the kids in the front room and drank a glass
of water to calm her nerves.

Getting dinner for Lily Solmonson, entertaining her
properly in our funny house with four kids and an irre-
pressible husband who painted thistles in the final moments
before the guests were to arrive was taking its toll. But when
the knock came, Mother thrust off her apron, patted her
hair and smiled brightly.

There they were, Mound City's handsomest couple, he in a dark well-pressed suit, Lily in a "simple" white cotton dress, placketed and pleated, tucked and rolled, not to mention embroidered, looking like a page right out of Delineator magazine. I could see Mother's eyes searching, the room, the kids, Dad, to make sure we were up to the occasion. No uncombed hair, snotty nose, drooly chin would do. Hastily she patted herself one more time to be sure the lace at her bosom was lying right, her hair was neat and the apron gone. The table looked fine, even the thistles added a nice note. Relieved she ushered us all to the table.

Lily was generous with her praise. The dinner was delicious, the table lovely, the children delightful. "Minnie, I just don't see how you do it all, four children, nice ones of course, a husband, this . . ."—she didn't know what to say about our ugly house—"and you invite company for dinner. I think it is wonderful. So brave of you!"

Mother blushed and then carried away with her pleasure said, "Oh it's nothing, I love to entertain and it is really no trouble."

We all looked at each other, Dad grinned and just then brother Bobby spoke up.

"We didn't had these dishes before. Does they belong to Kochs?" He had gone across the road with Mother to borrow May Koch's pretty water pitcher. Ours was broken.

Dad laughed for just a minute, there went Mother's pretense of frequent entertaining. Her youngest child didn't even recognize the company dishes. He needed to learn to watch his tongue, she thought. She was embarrassed, afraid Lily would think she had to borrow everything, dishes, tablecloth, napkins, everything. While it would have been a terrible disgrace to have a less than perfect party for Lily, it would be even worse to look like someone who would go to any lengths to impress her.

Dad spoke up quickly to say that Minnie was a marvel in the kitchen. "And I'm afraid I take advantage of her, bringing so many folks home to dinner."

He did. Every book salesman, farmer who came to town for tractor parts, applicant for a job teaching in a country school, stray shopper, anyone caught in town at dinner time, came home to eat at our table. Mother just whipped a clean tablecloth on the kitchen table, dragged an extra chair from the front room and dinner was ready. But she didn't count that as real company and it never occurred to her that her talent in that direction was of far more importance in her relationship with my father than what went on that night.

Lily Solmonson was not only pretty and sweet, she was honest in her praise of a woman who could take care of a house and kids, a garden, sew, wash and iron with no household amenities and still cook a wonderful meal and put on a show for company, but even more impressed that that woman could add at least one extra diner to her table any day of the week without turning a hair. The evening ended pleasantly and we all went on adoring Lily. Bobby leaned over from Dad's arms as the Solmonsons left the house and touched Lily's face. "You pwetty," he said. And in Lily's delight, even Mother forgot her former embarrassment.

Rain

⌒

SNOW I REMEMBER and icicles, chapped lips and chilblains, dusty heat that stung the nose and little rivulets of sweat that ran down backs and arms. And newborn spring mornings when the air turned from icy to soft, lambent warmth and first summer days that smelled of wild onions. I remember the autumn pungency of burning Russian thistles and I remember pure blue cloudless skies and high white fleecy clouds and dark threatening ones that menaced. But I hardly remember rain.

There was a picture in our primer of children clustered at a window, rain falling outside and the poem, "Rain, rain go away. Come again some other day," printed beneath it. Only once can I recall feeling as those children must have felt. It was Saturday, there was no school, as soon as my chores were done, I was free to explore the town, hunt up my friends, search the hilly pasture for wildflowers, tend my gopher traps. I was free and the world beckoned me to come and play.

My school clothes neatly hung and folded, breakfast dishes wiped, I rushed out the back door. Great wet drops caused little puffs of dust and the roof of the coal shed was shrouded in mist. Morning sun was disappearing in a fleet of gray and charcoal-colored clouds. My mother called to me to come in and just then lazy big drops turned to pelting, cold needles.

My father had gone to work but he would be home early. The two little boys were stretched out on the front room floor with their cars and trucks and Buster to provide mountains and hiding places so that they might speed around blind curves and crash into one another. In the kitchen Mother was mixing bread dough and my sister Kathleen was offering expert assistance. She could measure ingredients accurately and without spilling. When the bread was ready to set, they would start on doughnuts, a regular Saturday treat.

I thrust my head in between them to watch the process. "Watch your hair Elizabeth, we don't want hair in the bread," Mother cautioned. I climbed up on the chair across from her to settle myself on the edge of the table so I could see. "Get down, honey, there isn't room for you. The table might tip."

Disconsolately I wandered about. I turned my chair so I could peer out the small kitchen window and watch the streams course through the yard into the ditch in front of the house. Dust turned to mud before my eyes and little ponds formed in the road where the gravel had been thrown out by cars. My world had turned watery gray.

"Why don't you get your book and read," Mother suggested. I climbed onto the brown leather davenport and tried to get interested in the Bobbsey twins. For once Nan and Ned failed me. I listened to my brothers chuckle and turn their voices into thrumming motors, Buster's tail thumped the floor now and then. From the kitchen came the companionable voices of my mother and sister. It was too early for my father to come home. I was alone, the odd man out.

I dozed and woke to my father's voice. In the kitchen he was sitting at the table suggesting new ways my mother might embellish the loaves of bread that were rising. Russian peanuts perhaps sprinkled on top or cuts in the crust in which melted butter could be dribbled before baking. He examined the pans of cinnamon rolls closely. Was Mother sure there was enough cinnamon, sugar and butter. "You know how I like them."

Now the house had an electrical current running through it—like the crackling hum on the lines strung between big poles that ran beside the road when we drove far enough away from Mound City. It was always like that when my father came home. We were more alert, ready, waiting, although for what we couldn't say. It was exciting when he was there, but not very restful. He made you laugh, he sang songs, and he tested you.

"Let's see some long division," he challenged my sister. "How much is five times six, four times eight, three times nine," he checked my multiplication skills. "Spell Mississippi, Montana, Missouri."

Mother cleared the kitchen table and dished up dinner, oniony patties of yesterday's mashed potatoes, a double ring of spicy sausage, apple sauce, canned peas, cabbage slaw with vinegar and bacon and the last of last week's bread toasted in the oven. For dessert there were doughnuts still warm, crunchy with cinnamon and sugar or slick with powdered sugar.

Mother and Kathleen hastily washed and dried the dishes. Dad noted that the rain had stopped and sent me to get on my overshoes to protect my only shoes from mud, and out to fill the coal tub for evening and next morning. He would bring it in when I was finished, he said.

I lifted the tub onto the red wagon and hurried to fill it with big chunks and dust pans full of smaller stuff. When I was finished I was free. I stamped through the puddles and made my way down the driveway to the ditch where I watched the water riffle through the weeds. On the edge of the road was an ant hill, no ants. Where were they I wondered. Deep inside somewhere far beneath the crusty earth. I thought about gophers and mice and badgers and how they must hide in the darkness of their underground homes until the rain was over. Grasshoppers, where were they I wondered, and sparrows and blackbirds.

I walked toward town. At the post office where the wooden sidewalk started, I took off my overshoes, happy to rid myself of their weight and the clinking of their buckles. I hid them in the grass next to the building and walked on.

Adventures awaited me. Farmers would be in town with canvas roofs over their wagons. Eggs and cream must be sold and staples bought for the coming week. Maybe Willis could play, or Pauline. Maybe the red-headed blackbirds would be swinging on the reeds in the marsh at the edge of town. Maybe Johnny Solmonson would have candy in his pocket. Maybe—I loved that word, it meant anything was possible.

At home my father could read his paper in peace, my mother and the boys would take naps, my sister would follow her own desires. We would meet again when it turned dusk or the rain fell. There would be fresh bread and jam and fried potatoes for supper and sauce, peach maybe, or plums, and doughnuts. The world smelled clean and new, like my hair when it was shampooed, before the vinegar rinse. It was a new world, washed clean, full of promise, ready to give birth. It was mine.

Spring Cleaning

PRAIRIE WINTERS were long. It seemed to us they would never end. Sometimes we were teased by momentary lulls in the cold when the air turned soft and sucked little rivers from beneath the snow banks. For a few hours icicles dripped a steady plop-plop onto melting ground and grim skies softened. Then bitter cold returned and the wind keened and moaned around our thin-shelled houses. Icicles froze again, needle sharp, and the ground hardened.

One day, however, gentle rain washed away the last of the dirty snow, and the first green tips of thistle and prairie grass began to show. Rivulets of snow-melt and rain became coursing streams through tow-stubbing ground swells and ankle-deep mud bogs.

Soon the prairie bloomed with mayflowers and then bluebells and johnny-jump-ups and gumbo lilies. If you looked closely, you could find tiny blue star-flowers and the little white flowers of ground thistle. Summer would bring Indian paintbrush and sheep's fern.

Wild onions clamored for our attention, and no threat of expulsion saved the schoolroom from the sickening smell of wild onion breath. Eating them made me nauseated, but I ate. Perhaps we were starved for fresh greens after the long winter diet of canned vegetables, a few root crops left over from the last summer and sauerkraut. Whatever the reason, we punished ourselves and our friends and made life miserable for our teachers—we ate wild onions.

When we could finally be certain that spring was no passing fancy, the air remained warm and moist by day and only sharp at night. We shed the multi-layers of winter clothing and reveled in the freedom of lightly-covered bodies and bare feet. We spent hours searching the pastures for our favorite signs of the advancing season, watching gopher mounds and preparing our Christmas present gopher traps for our campaign. The tails of stripies brought two cents from the county and pocket gophers a nickel—a lot of money when penny candy was truly a penny.

Each day was golden until one fateful Sunday our mother would announce, "Tomorrow we will start spring cleaning." Those words brought naked fear to the eyes of children old enough for memory and resigned distaste to the faces of husbands. Women looked determined, challenged and in charge.

Escape was not possible. The next week would be a hell of scrubbing and scraping, hauling and tugging, and washing, starching, and polishing.

Before daylight Monday morning, after the wash was hung, beds were dismantled, springs and mattresses hauled out to the yard to be scrubbed, pummeled and aired until just before supper. Mother scanned the skies with worried eyes for an errant cloud. Emergency signals for help must be sounded if rain threatened.

While beds aired, floors were scrubbed and polished. Carpets were carried to the clothesline to be beaten within an inch of their lives. Curtains came down to soak in a tub of Fels Naptha suds. They would be rinsed and starched and stretched to the breaking point before they were rehung.

We trooped home for noon dinner to find spartan fare, warmed-over soup perhaps, and canned fruit. Weary Mother, her hair tied up in an old diaper or stuffed into a dust cap, sipped a cup of tea and marshaled her forces. "Kathleen, give the Brussels carpet another whack or two. Elizabeth, carry in the rag rugs. Den, when can you get the storm windows down and the screens up? We'll want the storm doors off too." Happily we slunk back to our schoolrooms and office, but we knew what to expect when we got home again. And home we had better get the minute we were dismissed.

In the next few days every inch of wall and woodwork, every shelf and cupboard was scrubbed and waxed or varnished. Every drawer was turned out, winter bedding was aired and washed and stored away in mothballs. Our winter clothing shared the trunks and boxes—when the season changed we would all smell of mothballs for weeks.

The front room coal stove was carried out to the coalshed where it sat until one late summer day it would be scraped clean and blacked, the chrome shined, ready to return to its place of honor when the season changed. The front room floor was rubbed to a slippery shine. Finally the windows were polished and the summer drapes of flowered cretonne showed up at the windows, and flowered pillow shams camouflaged the winter-weary sofa cushions. The outhouse was cleaned and deodorized, the root cellar emptied and aired. The whole place took on the odor of strong soap, Lysol and ammonia.

Saturday brought the last great gasps of energy and the last meal of bread and scraps and canned stuff. That night our weekly baths took on new meaning. Tomorrow we would march to church, clean inside and out, victorious, celebrating our fight against dirt and sloth, secure in the knowledge that if cleanliness was next to godliness, we were mighty close.

And we went home to pot roast and apple pie. And, by golly, there would be succulent hash for supper, maybe with an egg. Dad looked happy, Mother relaxed. Even the dog appeared from his hiding place under the house.

Sunshine's Season

N OW THE AIR was full of the smell of green growing things and we reveled in the warm dirt under our bare feet. Dirt that had not yet turned to dry dust but kept just a whisper of dampness left from spring rains. Sun bathed our bare shoulders and arms and we were allowed to wear our old overalls so many times washed and sun dried that only soft lightness touched our skin. Looking back it seems as if the sun stood high in the sky for more hours than could have been possible. I remember a world suffused with sunshine.

Spring cleaning was done and it was too early for canning. In the fields spring plowing and planting were over and crops were growing green and fertile. There was no worry yet about a too dry summer, The cows had calved and leggy lambs gamboled in the meadows. Newly-born pigs were beginning to fatten. There was only the cultivating of fields and garden to worry about, the animals to be fed and fattened. Milking, of course, and egg gathering were relentless chores on the farm, but all in all it was a slightly relaxed time, where women and farmers could take a little breather and prepare for the toil ahead.

These were the days when we spent hours playing in the grove, a small acreage deeded to the town by a generous citizen as a recreation area. Here we hunted wild flowers, made daisy chains, and put on mock weddings. No boy would join us for that activity, so one of the bigger girls tucked her shirt into her black bloomers and put on a father's hat that had been sneaked out in spite of a mother's watchful eyes. The groom was ready. A borrowed lace curtain was placed on the bride's head and pinned with a circlet of wild flowers. Someone with the gift of words was chosen to be the minister, alas I was too young and too short. The rest of us were flower girls, ushers and weeping parents of the couple. Before we were through with the ceremony we were usually rolling in the grass laughing at the minister's jumble of Bible verses, advice to the bride and groom and the order to "kiss the bride." Usually the groom would grab the poor girl and bend her so far back that although you could see that their heads were together you couldn't tell that their lips weren't touching. We didn't believe in girls kissing girls.

The Blauert girls, their father was minister of the Lutheran Church, celebrated their birthdays by dressing up as brides and inviting their party guests to accompany them in a parade down Main Street. I was always green with envy—I wanted to be a bride, all dressed in the lacy costume their ingenious mother put together with odds and ends of household decoration. I suspect I clumped along behind the bride scowling my disapproval but I hung in there lest I miss the cake and lemonade.

There is a picture in the family album of me as the

bride in a Tom Thumb wedding. I don't remember these events although I must have been three at the time. Willis Kolodzie was the groom and we both were decked out in traditional wedding finery, I in a frilly white lace dress with coronet and veil. Willis wore a tiny tuxedo.

Producers of these events made the rounds of small towns flattering parents and wooing merchants to put up the money for their time and costumes. Admissions were charged, and most of the money left town with them. But the country folk all came to town on a Saturday to do their shopping and stayed for the "wedding" that evening. Many a family album carries the record of that event. The year Willis and I were the happy couple one photo showed him with unbuttoned trousers and a bit of flesh showing where it oughtn't to have. I imagine there was a good deal of suppressed laughter and it was one of the more successful evenings. I remember seeing the photo, but some time later it disappeared. Mother must have thought it was too unseemly.

Now that school was over, if we ran out of other things to do, we set up a schoolroom in the shade of the Methodist Church or someone's still green lilac bush and took turns being teacher and students. We read and wrote and did arithmetic and we all took advantage of our turn to be teacher by being as bossy as we had ever wanted to be. Of course, if the bigger girls were playing with us, people my size didn't get to be teacher. We docilely stood in the corner, held out our hands to be smacked and then complained loudly, "Ow, that's too hard." Occasionally one of us went home crying or several of us departed in a huff to find other amusement.

These were long, sweet days. Evenings my parents sometimes drove us north of town a short way to Spring Creek and we were allowed to paddle and swim in its still

Denny & Minnie Mills c. 1915

Elizabeth at 18 months of age.

It's not easy having a younger sister—Elizabeth (age 18 months) and Kathleen (age 4).

Left: Elizabeth and Grandma Kusler c. 1921

Grandma Kusler's house before the addition of the widow's walk.

*Main Street, Mound City
c. 1902*

Methodist Church

Mound City Schoolhouse

*Campbell
County
Courthouse,
Mound City,
South Dakota*

77

Winter was a time of bundling up against the chill.

Kathleen and Elizabeth in their beaver hats and plush coats.

*Elizabeth (age 4) and her
snowman.*

*Kathleen, Elizabeth
and friends.*

*The Mills children in front of the
only spruce tree in town,
c. 1925–26.*

Chester and Lily Solomonson (left and above).

Below: The Model T.

flowing waters. The two little boys waded creekside. Once while my mother and father both became occupied with one of us, someone turned to see baby brother Bob, barely able to toddle, face down in the water, his little diapered behind sticking up. Dad snatched him up and held him upside down to get rid of any water he had inhaled and burst into tears when the baby let out a wail at the rough treatment. When Mother grabbed him and crooned and cradled him in her arms he turned on a beatific smile. Told that the swim was over for that evening, we made no protest but gratefully climbed into the Model T for the ride home.

Summer blew in on a hot wind. Spring's soft cloudy skies turned brilliant with summer's hot sun and the horizon was a clear, hard edge. As far as we could see, and on the prairie that is a long, long way, there was hardly a pool of shade, rarely a cloud shadow. Only occasionally a black cloud would roar in on the ever present prairie wind turned howling monster and we would scan the skies for signs of cyclone and worry about hail. Sometimes heat lightning stabbed the sky, mostly it was just hot day after hot day; the outhouse grew pungent, Russian thistle thorns were dry and sharp.

Garden greens turned yellow and crackly despite evening after evening of lugging pails of water up and down the rows. the dust mixed with our sweat as my sister and I, armed with tin cans with a small amount of kerosene in them, worked our ways listlessly dragging up and down the paths picking off potato bugs and cabbage worms.

We lived outdoors, we kids, playing endless hours the childhood games that every prairie kid knew. We made grasshoppers spit tobacco, we played aunty-I-over, throwing a ball over a shed roof and for some reason I have forgotten, shouting "pigtail" at intervals. Duck on a rock and

King of the Mountain and Pom Pom Pull Away were favorites and we hauled our wash boiler boats to a pasture pond where we sailed under skull and crossbones, scaring the ducks and sometimes tipping over so that we had to put our bare feet into the squishy bottom.

Mother shipped me off to our grandparents, who lived in a little town twenty seven miles away, to lighten her load a bit. I loved going there, Grandma cooked my favorite foods and let me hunt for eggs in the barn. Grandpa squirted milk into my mouth when he milked the cow, let me play with the calf and tucked me into his Ford for long rides into the country to visit farms where he bought cattle and grain. Almost no one spoke English on the streets of Artas, their home town, but I had friends and two cousins who lived there so I did not lack for playmates. One summer my friend Jeanette and I dug baby turnips in her family's garden and walked around town selling them to amused neighbors.

Many a hot summer day we idled in the creek which had turned sluggish in the summer heat. We floated and swam a little, but much of the time we were simply quiet, squatting so that water covered our shoulders, and we talked and laughed away the day, only emerging periodically to tear off the leaches that attached to our bodies. We hated them; they were repulsive and painful but somehow our attraction to water, flowing water which was so rare in our lives, overcame our revulsion.

With the neighbor kids we played circus using the chickens, ducks, and calves in our show. We caught water snakes in the creek and garter snakes in the grass around it. I was the snake charmer, and I really thought I was a charmer, although my sister and several of her contemporaries were nauseated by my performance.

Only once I allowed myself to take part in a snake slaughter and helped to tie the snake around the barbed wire fence to see if he (or she) would wiggle until sundown as we had been told. When everyone else wandered away forgetting the reason for this horrible deed, I sat crying as the snake twisted and struggled. I didn't know what else to do, how to stop the apparent suffering, we had already cut off its head. I can still see that snake tied to a strand of pasture fence. I still feel the pain and shame at sitting there in the hot dusty grass, honor bound to wait for the last signs of life. I still mourn.

Night after summer night, my sister Kathleen and I rushed out after supper with admonitions to be home by dark. At summer's peak it could be as late as nine thirty before we had to share the evening with fireflies. These were the best of times when we played everyone's favorite game, Run Sheep Run. Divided into teams we roamed the whole town, one team hiding, the other seeking. An emissary from the hiding sheep visited the hunters, drew them a map of the location of their quarry and then accompanied them hollering signals which meant move or double back, to head north toward Deiberts or east toward the schoolhouse and finally calling out Run Sheep Run, which sent the sheep hurrying back to home base trying to beat the hunters. We took turns being sheep and hunters and the highest honor was to be named emissary, I think we called them scouts. How we plotted to save our team and to outwit the hunters. How proud we were at success; how important it was to hear comforting words, "Hey, you came close. Good try," if we lost. Wearily we dragged ourselves home, washed the dust from our bare feet at the pump, and tumbled into bed.

One day we came into the house looking for food to

find Mother counting fruit jars, quarts and pints lined up and, despite the heat, the wash boiler bubbling away on the coal range. Hell could have no fury worse than canning season in the summer heat.

We were captured. When the jars were boiled, peaches, pears, plums, whatever the fruit, were scalded, pitted or peeled, and stuffed into burning hot jars, then covered with steaming sugar syrup and laced with cinnamon sticks.

There were long days like this. Every vegetable had to be cleaned and blanched, peas shelled, green beans strung and then sealed into jars and boiled—it seemed like hours— to kill the threat of botulism. Soon fruits, vegetables and pickles, dill pickles, at least forty or fifty quarts, sweet ones, always pints, bread and butter, mustard, watermelon, crab apple and peach pickles lined the groaning shelves. Finally came chowchow, piccalilli and End of the Garden relishes to fill any empty spaces.

We moaned and groaned that we were too tired to wash and peel any more fruit or vegetables or rinse any more jars at the pump, and it was too hot, and we didn't need, couldn't possibly eat, all of this largesse. Mother just said, "I never see anyone complain when we open up a jar for supper in winter."

Despite canning and potato bugs, summer with the croak of frogs, the whine of mosquitoes, fireflies lighting the dark was a perfect time. But then we began to think about the joys of autumn and then of the winter ahead. There was always something just as wonderful as the day we were in, to look forward to.

The Whistling Jacket

I T WAS EARLY SUMMER—a warm-cool day. The sun felt
friendly on my shoulders but I kept my jacket, the green
and brown striped one, buttoned tight against the breeze
that searched insistently for a way to get inside.

It was scratchy, but it was my favorite jacket. My mother
made it out of an old lightweight wool shirt of my grandpa's.
She made almost all of our clothes, except my father's. You
couldn't make shoes, so she let us go barefoot a lot. Mostly
she used the cast off clothing of our friends and relatives as
material which she meticulously cleaned and pressed and
then she cut a paper pattern and patiently altered, tucked
and hemmed until the garment fit. She wanted her family
to look nice, neat and attractive, and she was not oblivious
to style. Much of what we wore was patterned after the pictures in the Sears or "Monkey" Ward catalogues and she
followed the advice of the children's fashion pages in the
women's magazines of the day.

For Christmas or a birthday we might get new material. That's how I got my red wool dress with the embroidery on the yoke and sleeves. Santa Claus brought it. But Mrs. Santa didn't have time to finish it, my mother said, and she would do it just as soon as she could. I wore it a long time and cried when finally there wasn't any more hem to let out and I had to walk with my shoulders hunched forward because it was so tight. I begged Mother not to give it away—not yet. I couldn't bear to part with the soft red wool and the garlands of blue and green and violet flowers. That dress made me feel beautiful. The jacket made me feel grown up, and important. Like maybe a little bit of Grandpa rubbed off on me.

Mother was busy in the house that morning and my chores were finished. It must have been Saturday since I was six and wasn't in school. I slipped the jacket over my overalls and my underwear top and sidled out the back door. I didn't want to be called back to wash my face or put on a different shirt. I was in a hurry.

I had learned to walk gingerly to avoid splinters on the wooden sidewalk that ran along our road past the post office and joined up with the one on Main Street right in front of the Mercantile.

I usually searched carefully for a penny that might have rolled between the sidewalk boards or stopped to study the tracks a garter snake must have made in the dust. I almost always caught a grasshopper and got him to spit tobacco. But not this day. I was oblivious to the lacy-leafed boxelder tree and didn't bother to pick up even the prettiest stone, flecked with mica, that could have joined the collection in my secret hidey hole behind the outhouse.

I was trying desperately to learn to whistle—had been for days. It seemed the most important thing in the world to me and I could imagine myself bringing an audience to its feet in amazed wonderment at my rendition of *Believe Me if All Those Endearing Young Charms* at the next home talent show. Certainly I would put those big boys in the third and fourth grades in their places. They would never make fun of me again.

Pucker and blow, pucker and blow, I squinched my eyes and rolled my tongue with concentration. After all this time the best I could do was a weak little rasp, something like a very sick, very small mouse might have made as it gasped its last breath.

Joe Alexander who owned the Mercantile and was father to a playmate, Martha Jane, saw me as I paused in front of the store. I liked to stand there when customers opened and closed the door. In the rush of air it made, I caught the smell of all the things inside, penny candy and turpentine and woolen underwear. And sweeping compound and fly paper and Johannes Brot—its odor was unforgettable and it was used as a medicine by some people. The same people, I expect, who tied noxious asafetida bags around their kids' necks and made them swallow monstrous doses of sulfur and molasses as a spring tonic every year. My parents stuck to the oils, our daily cod liver oil and castor oil when it was called for. The very thought of that oily dosing and the ensuing griping pain and frequent trots to the outhouse usually accomplished the necessary trick without further action.

Joe Alexander was my hero, one of several I admired in our little town. That day he stepped out into the breezy sunshine to encourage my whistling efforts. "You'll get it, you'll get it—keep going," he said. And he puckered and pursed his lips and pressed his tongue against his teeth to demonstrate the proper technique. Then he patted me on the shoulder and went back into the store.

I retraced my steps and took shelter behind the pile of last year's Russian thistles in the vacant lot next to our house. The dusty ground was comfortably warm and I felt confident my mother wouldn't notice me there if she came out to shake the rugs or empty the scrub pail. I puckered and blew and blew and puckered and suddenly there it was, a whistle. A full blown, respectably long drawn out whistle—the way I remembered Grandpa whistling when he went out to feed the dog. The glorious sound sent me galloping, jacket billowing in the wind, around the lot until I was sure I had the process under control. Then I ran off down the hill to demonstrate to Joe. He grinned and danced around, weaving and waving clenched fists like a victorious boxer, and handed me a congratulatory chocolate drop.

Whistling bravely, and loudly, I showed up at home for noon dinner eager to entertain my parents, my sister and two little brothers with my prowess. As that day and then days and weeks wore on, there were fewer congratulations and more sh-sh-shs. But from then on, my piercing whistle accompanied music on the radio, *The Star Spangled Banner* and *America, the Beautiful* at the Fourth of July celebration, and I had to be shushed with a firm grip on my shoulder to keep me quiet through the hymns at church on Sunday.

I learned to whistle softly under the covers at night when I couldn't sleep and to hide in the outhouse to practice when I was banned from the house unless I promised silence for the rest of the day. For a long time, no matter the temperature, I grabbed that green jacket when I went outside to practice. I thought it had a kind of magic which would help me to whistle the way my grandpa did and it seemed to me I whistled best when I was wearing it.

Picnics at the River

〜

IT WAS AN ANXIOUS TIME of hard work on the prairie. Farm
ers cultivated and eyed the skies hoping for just the right
amount of rain at the right time and looked forward to the
harvest. Women everywhere began the arduous summer
long job of "canning up" the garden. The Mason jars were
hauled out of their many hiding places and my sister and I
were set to work clearing them of spider webs and giving
them a first washing under the backyard pump. Next they
were washed again in clean, hot soapy water and finally
rinsed and then boiled in the copper wash boilers ready to
be stuffed with beans and peas and tomatoes, and late late
in the season, sweet corn. Cucumbers picked in the early
morning cool were soaked in cold well water until they
tested crisp enough to be put down in brine, heavily flavored with dill and pickling spices.

Women vied with each other to produce the most colorful, sparkling jars of vegetables, fruits and pickles. There
were quarts and quarts of "sauce" to help relieve the mo-

notony of winter meals when fresh produce could neither
be grown nor bought.

This orgy of cleaning, blanching, boiling and pickling
of fruits and vegetables went on until very late summer. All
through the "dog days" of August when it was said that dogs
went mad from the oppressive heat, our kerosene stove
turned the kitchen into a hell hole and I worried that my
mother's flushed face would never recover its usual pretty
color. Sometimes even the coal stove was fired up despite
the temperature—there was much to do. Clothes still had
to be scrubbed and boiled and ironed. The hungry family
had to be fed, bread baked and pies and cakes furnished
for family desserts and Ladies Aid suppers. It was summer-
time, but the living was not easy for prairie folks.

But these were wise men and women. They set aside
time for the joys of summer and that meant picnics at the
river. The Fourth of July often heralded the beginning of
this season, and on the day before, gardens were left to
their own devices and stoves were fired up to fry great tubs
of chicken and boil potatoes for salad. Early next morning,
Model T Fords and flivvers of every kind, even buggies and
farm wagons were loaded with food and kids, and extra
clothes and blankets to sit on, old sheets for tablecloths,
croquet sets, balls, bats, inner tubes and a mighty procession left town to meet farm families along the way for the
long drive to the river. One of the traditions upon which
we insisted was a stop to open the farm gate we crossed to
get to the river and my father would demonstrate to us the
magic of the natural gas "spring" beside it by lighting a
match and setting the water that bubbled up on fire.

This was summer heaven, one of the year's high spots
that ranked with Christmas and Thanksgiving as celebrations. It was extra special because fathers helped with fire-

crackers and sparklers. Mothers nursed burned fingers and broken hearts when only the big kids were allowed to light the roman candles. What I loved most were the little strings of baby firecrackers—you lit one and moved away and the whole string went off, one by one, dancing in the dust. My father was always hovering close to supervise, to be sure we used a punk stick instead of matches, to keep our sparklers away from each other and our fire crackers in the safe dirt rings provided.

If it wasn't too early for watermelons, they were set in the river to cool. Ice cream freezers were wrapped in wet gunny sacks so they would stay icy and the men built cooking fires with dead cottonwood limbs and set grates across hastily assembled stone fireplaces to boil corn. The women unloaded and unwrapped the treasures from their kitchens and cellars.

"Try this piccalilli, it's a new recipe."

"I put these little sweet onions instead of carrots in my dill this year. What do you think?"

"Oh, there's Alma's coconut cream cake—get it in the shade. I want a piece of that."

Husbands relaxed from storekeeping and road work, from judging and banking, from milking and plowing to swing at softballs and hunt for wild grapes along the river, laughing and comparing notes about life. And kids raced around chasing each other and the dogs who had been invited until they were admonished to "stop raising so much dust around the tables."

"You can go wade in the river but don't you go past the big log there. Now hear me? Your daddy will take you swimming pretty soon."

And we did swim. We ate prodigiously and played in the dusty grass. Dad and Mr. Larsen officiated at three legged races and sack races while the women with only a little help from husbands and children, filled every empty food container and syrup pails brought for the purpose with tiny wild grapes, chokecherries and buffalo berries for more jelly to be cooked up in their hot kitchens in the days that followed.

There were speeches too, sometimes the Judge, sometimes Dad or someone from the American Legion, all about Independence Day and what it meant and how important it was to celebrate together and remember what it took to get us free and how we mustn't forget. And there were songs—all the things we could sing without a piano. If there was a mouth organ we sang to that. I liked *America* about how God shed his Grace on thee. I could see golden rays coming down from God to light us up right there along the Missouri River in South Dakota.

There was always a second eating, kids were allowed to run around with a drumstick and bread and butter, and later with chunks of watermelon in which we buried our faces and gobbled right down to the rind, even as we were being reminded not to eat the green. "You'll get a stomach ache." By this time kids were getting cranky, mothers worn and farmers thinking about the milking, feeding and egg gathering that awaited them at home.

At last the return procession was under way, dirty dishes and the fruit and leftovers were packed in with kids and dogs. Garbage had been carefully buried, fires checked to be sure they were out—it was time to go home. We didn't insist on seeing the burning spring again, but called tired goodnights to families that dropped off along the way. Before long most of us were asleep, moms and dads alert and careful to see us safely home.

Bedtime preparations were hasty that night, still sleeping babies plunked into cribs, mosquito bites daubed with alcohol, sunburned faces dabbed with vinegar and coated with Vaseline and lights were extinguished. For a few hours the town was dark and then one by one a lamp was lit, a sick child escorted to the outhouse or held over a chamber pot. Sunburns had to be treated once more, babies changed, drinks of water distributed before weary parents could sink back into their beds. Next morning women gossiped over clotheslines and party lines and men met on the street, still tired, another picnic the last thing anyone wanted to think about. But before long, the thrill of water running, big trees, a chance for the whole town to be together once again before winter would beckon and the word around town would be, "See you Sunday. What time shall we start?"

Oh, Elizabeth

THE ICE CREAM STORE in Mound City was also the candy store and the pool room. We didn't say pool hall, that sounded too vulgar. I always thought of it as the ice cream parlor although it didn't have ice cream except when it was trucked in on Saturday afternoon every other week. Since we had no electricity in town, there was no way to have a regular supply of anything that required freezing.

There were the two or three requisite spindly, largely unused, twisted wire tables and chairs in the store and a candy counter that displayed a few dusty chocolates, hand dipped by Mrs. Kolodzie, I think. We never could afford those but once in awhile during the time that Willis Kolodzie was my best friend, I was treated to a chocolate drop.

Somehow my parents always managed to come up with the required coins so we could have an ice cream treat the Saturdays that the truck came to town with a ration of the delicious stuff. You could smell tobacco and hear men's voices and the click of balls while you waited. There was always just one flavor, vanilla, with chocolate sprinkles or without—that was the extent of your choice. But my goodness what a treat it was to nibble and lick at the mound of creamy ivory colored goodness, catching it as it ran down our sleeves in the summer heat. Eat it fast was our motto, never mind your manners. And when the very last bit of frozen cream was pushed down into the tiny piece of cone left, we'd bite off the bottom and suck the final succulent drops and then pop the remnant of wafer into our mouths, happy that we hadn't lost a drop, but crushed that the delicacy was gone, not to be replaced for another two weeks. When my mother helped me strip for the Saturday night bath in the tin wash tub, she would peel the sticky clothes away and note my cream streaked arms. As I bent to lick the stuff, "Oh Elizabeth," she always said.

We were just like all the other kids—no matter what delicious desserts our mother whipped up for us, apple pie, angel food cake, peach cobbler, it was the one we couldn't have for which we lusted. Oh, we ate her daily homemade treats with gusto, but we still dreamed of that far away Saturday when the ice cream truck would come again.

The only people in town who had an ice house were the Nostes who owned the grocery/dry goods store. They also owned a truck and had two husky sons who could go to the river and cut ice and haul it home. In the ice house it was covered with great piles of straw to keep it frozen and when you got invited to the Nostes, maybe for a Sunday afternoon visit, one requirement, mine at least, was to be allowed to peek into the ice house and smell the melting rivery smell mixed with the dry sweet smell of clean straw.

We would be seated in the parlor with our parents and the Noste family with big bowls of ice cream to hold and from which to eat with lady-like little bites. Theirs was a lovely house, furnished with dark woods and carpets and presided over by Mrs. Noste. I remember her as a pale, slender woman, already gray, with a very soft voice and piercing eyes. I knew she was a lady with every nuance of meaning that word held. The thought of dribbling ice cream or eating too fast, of doing anything but sitting decorously, a perfect lady myself, was unbearable. Consequently, I could never finish my ice cream. The strain was too much—I was too afraid I might spill, too aware of the sound of my lips opening and closing and the clink of my spoon against the delicate china dish. I couldn't wait to be excused to go outdoors and roll in the grass, visit the cowshed, sniff the flowers, anything to get rid of the terrible tension I felt as the result of a very generously meant invitation to share their frozen treat. My mother would shake her head apologetically and then release me with the words, "Oh Elizabeth, run on."

Homemade ice cream in those days was truly cream, with a custard base and quarts and quarts of whipping cream. It was so rich that even if I had not been worried about my behavior, I would never have been able to finish a whole bowl. A few teaspoonfuls, three or four at the most, and I began to feel the beginnings of a sickish, overfed feeling that came to me with even small amounts of the very rich, sweet, vanilla flavored ice cream.

The only time we could make our own ice cream was in the winter. Sometimes we made something we called snow cream. It required very cold weather and deep clean snow. We mixed our ice cream base, a little like an eggnog I think, and then poured it onto a patch of clean snow where it was supposed to congeal and take on a resemblance to ice cream. It didn't much. But it was sweet and the process was entertaining so we did it as often as we could talk Mother out of the required ingredients. Pestered until she could withstand us no longer she would give in, making her way to pantry and kitchen table around my dancing impatience until she would finally trip and explode, "Oh, Elizabeth!"

The other way we could have winter ice cream was to freeze a couple of pails of water on a cold night and then use the ice in our wooden ice cream freezer with plenty of rock salt to make it colder. But somehow, winter nights were made more for taffy pulling or making fudge or penuche— the candies we all loved. On Friday nights I would begin my pleading for a candy making session. I would do all the work, I insisted, and clean up too. Remembering other Fridays my mother would rise and begin assembling the ingredients murmuring in painful patience, "Oh Elizabeth."

We didn't fool around with anything like a candy thermometer but depended on our ability to judge when the confection was ready to be removed from the stove and beaten by when it reached just the right stage of firmness, soft ball it was called, in a cup of cold water. And then beat we did, for hours it seemed to me whose skinny wrists gave out after a lick or two. Mother beat and Kathleen and finally, if necessary, Dad took a turn. Then the lucious stuff was mixed with a cup of toasted walnuts and poured onto a pie plate to be set out on the snow so it would hurry and cool and be ready to eat. Each time I went out to check its readiness, I took a swipe with my finger so when the plate was finally brought in for everyone to share, my mother took one look and said, "Oh, Elizabeth."

Taffy was less of a favorite, but we did find the pulling part fun. With our buttery hands we would pull and fold the stuff back together again, pull and fold, until it was shiny and almost impossible to stretch. Then it went into the pie pan and out to cool. Sometimes it got so hard the only way we could eat it at all was to suck it for hours.

I was known to wake in the morning, a glob of taffy and carmelly juice stuck to my nightclothes. Oh yes, I had brushed my teeth, I assured Mother while she was putting the little boys to bed. Oh yes, I had, but then I popped a wad of taffy back into my mouth, sweetness to see me through the night.

Mother examined her sticky second child and announced that just as soon as she had time, we would have to wash my hair. A shampoo didn't fit into her heavy schedule, hauling and heating the water, setting newspapers about to protect her clean floor, soaping and rinsing over the washbasin to the tune of my cries of "Soap, soap in my eyes." Finally she would fling me a towel and let her exasperation ring out in the words, "Oh, Elizabeth!"

The Little Brown Church

⟋⟍

THE FACT THAT WE LIVED right next door to the Methodist church may have had something to do with it. And the fact that my father loved to sing and his quartet often sang for Sunday services probably had an influence. But mostly it was just "done," whether you were religious or not, going to church was as much a part of life as going to work and school or brushing your teeth. Practically everybody did it.

I don't remember Sunday School in the Methodist Church in Mound City. If we had it and I went, it made little impression. I barely remember a minister delivering a sermon. I did of course have some opinions about matters religious, I had opinions about practically everything. I thought Jesus was probably a pretty nice person, a sort of older brother who wore funny clothes and let his hair grow long, hair the color of wheat. My father said he was probably a lot darker than his pictures, but that didn't affect his goodness. I tried to imagine him walking around barefoot in his long nightshirt with a piece of rope around his waist. But I must say I was put off by the fact that it didn't seem to me that he accomplished very much. People were still mean to each other, some parents hit their kids, and perfectly nice people fell on hard times. I was sure he felt sorry about all that and tried hard to make people better, talking about things like "Do unto others" and that stuff.

As for God, well, I wasn't too favorably impressed with him either. Except when I got in trouble and without thinking started to pray. "Oh God, just don't let Mother find out I was the one who stole the last piece of fudge and I'll never, never do it again," I'd whisper to myself.

But I still pretty much liked to go to church and I can still feel the smooth wooden hardness of the pews when you ran your hands over the arms or the seats. The hymn books always gave off a slightly musty aroma and you could smell sweeping compound and furniture polish and oftentimes early in winter there was the faint odor of mothballs that shook out from winter coats and women's dresses. Sometimes when it was hot, you could smell lilac water or the heavily rose scented pomade that a few men wore to keep their hair in order.

The Methodist Church was a plain building, brown mostly, boasting nothing like stained glass windows, but when the sun came through the plain ones it turned the dust motes into diamonds and sparkled on people's glasses. There was a constant rustling of women's dresses, children moving impatiently, hymn book pages turning and men surreptitiously loosening the stiff collars of their gleaming starched shirts.

All this quiet noise came to a sudden stop when the music started. I loved the quartet's renditions of some of the more obscure hymns, but what transported us all, set us swaying on our feet, heads up, voices released to the maximum, was the congregation singing together. Young and old, we raised our voices in *Bringing in the Sheaves,* we gathered by the river, and we marched in place to *Onward Christian Soldiers.* But it was *The Little Brown Church* that was my favorite and Hattie Allen's booming voice as she sang "Oh come, come, come to the little brown church in the wildwood, the little brown church in the vale." I always tried to sit where I could watch her sing, her great contralto voice soaring out of fussy Sunday dress up clothes, rusty black taffeta with a high collar I seem to remember, and a little capelet around her shoulders and over her mighty bosom. But the voice, the voice rollicked and soared, it challenged and defied, it led you and you sang too, the whole congregation boomed along with Hattie until the last word of the last song had been sung.

We sank to our seats, exhausted, but cleansed, our burdens happily lifted. Then we rose to ring out the words of the benediction and the final amen. Hands were shaken all around, kids darted among parent's skirts and trousers, but our thoughts were now of dinner waiting at home, baking or simmering on the coal range. Sometimes roast beef or pork on a bed of sauerkraut or crusty chicken fried early that morning. These were usually accompanied by mashed potatoes and thick dark brown gravy and maybe a jar of Mother's home canned peas or green beans smothered in cream and butter. If it was pot roast, the potatoes would be browned to a deep mahogany along with the meat and carrots and onions in a tightly covered dutch oven. And there would be pie, there was always pie on Sunday. Cake was for some other day; we liked our apple or peach or berry or apricot or pumpkin or, oh, best of all, Grandma's sour cream raisin pie with cinnamon and allspice and cloves and just a touch, a mere whiff of vinegar. On Sunday, it had to be pie.

Logy with food, my sister and I stuporously wiped the dishes Mother washed in one dishpan and rinsed in the other set on the old oak kitchen table. And then she retired to the brown leather davenport in the front room to nap while Dad reclined with his feet on the footstool in the matching rocker to read the paper. Kids were free to do whatever we wanted, quietly. Sometimes we sat at the kitchen table and played paper dolls or Uncle Wiggly, or I pulled a pillow down to the floor where I would lie and read fairy tales or Elsie Dinsmore. Often we slept, briefly, lightly, afraid to miss anything.

Sooner or later, we roused from the results of our heavy noon meal and headed outdoors to join our friends and play whatever game the season dictated. In winter we dragged out our sleds, in summer we joined in a game of Pom Pom Pullaway, Duck on the Rock, or our favorite, Run Sheep Run. If it was too hot, we aimlessly jostled one another, sharing drinks at someone's pump, maybe teeter tottering or swinging at the schoolhouse. What counted was that we were together, our good churchy feelings of happy singing still with us and we were reluctant to part when our parents' voices sounded calling us home for supper.

A Garden's Secret

I LOVED TO VISIT MRS. KOSEL. Sometimes my mother or Martha would send me to her to get onions or potatoes or dill, then I would skip across the dusty gravel road and find her in her garden and she would invite me in. In winter, I watched for her trips to the coal shed and the outhouse and hailed her when she headed back to her house.

Although I schemed to get her attention, I was always momentarily tongue-tied and awkward when Mrs. Kosel smiled her gentle elfin smile and bid me welcome. She spoke a heavily accented mixture of German and English in which every sentence sounded like a question. Weekdays she was always dressed in long dark dresses with long sleeves and light gray aprons. She wore dark gray bonnets which tied under her chin. On Sundays, the dress and bonnet were black and the apron white, very modestly trimmed with white embroidery. Her weekday high-tops were heavy brown work shoes which she exchanged for polished, worn, black ones for Sunday.

Years later, I saw my first dried apple doll and said to myself, "That's Mrs. Kosel." Her probably once rosy face had seamed and dried into wrinkles, lumps and caverns, heavily shadowed by the brim of her bonnet. I could not imagine how she had looked as a young woman.

I do not remember that she ever joined in the life of the small town, was seen at socials, picnics or school programs. Little children shied away from her and big ones whispered that she was a witch. At first I thought she might be. Her chin was too long and her nose hooked down as if to meet it. But once I strayed past her gate on a dusty summer day and she held out to me some tender green peas. I stood a moment, shelling and eating the green fruit and followed when she beckoned me to enter her little gray house.

Mostly I remember how cool it seemed after the hot, late summer afternoon outdoors. And the smell. The smell of dill and vinegar, onions and cabbage. Sheaves of herbs and dried corn hung from the ceiling and baskets of vegetables lined the walls, carrots and onions, squash and cabbage. There were great crocks of pickles and sauerkraut. Here I was introduced to the smell of garlic and little spicy peppers.

The only rooms I ever saw were the kitchen and the dark little parlor, which I remember as a dim, low-ceilinged room with a wooden rocker and a pie crust table which bore her spectacles and a huge German Bible. In these little rooms, Mrs. Kosel lived out her life. Except for Sunday services at the Lutheran church and an occasional errand to the drygoods store on Main Street, she stayed at home. There she cooked and dried and preserved the food she raised in her garden, read and cleaned, sewed, and dozed her life away in the fragrant little house. She did, that is, except when she was tending her little flock of hens or working in her garden where old-fashioned flowers vied for space with the herbs and vegetables on which she survived.

I don't recall anyone else visiting her. I didn't know of any family and I didn't even wonder about a Mr. Kosel. I didn't tell my friends about my visits and I did not ask my parents questions about her. I was not curious about who she was or had been or where she came from. It was enough for me that she smiled, murmured garden and cooking lore in her polyglot language, and gave me tastes of delicious food. She existed, I must have thought, for me. She was my fairy tale outside a book, my secret character. I would not have been surprised to find out that she was an enchantress, a real princess waiting for magic to restore her to youth and beauty. But I would not have been disappointed to learn that she was the old peasant woman who befriended the great gray wolf. Indeed, I loved her just as Mrs. Kosel, my secret friend, in her secret little house in her secret little garden. I still visit her there.

Lost at the Fair

MOSTLY I REMEMBER dust and heat and people, more people than I had ever seen. Their knees are what I remember because that is what I saw, a lot of moving legs and knees that bent and shoes of course—big ones. My mother clutched my hand and kept looking down at me nervously and then somehow I was loose, no hand holding mine, being pressed forward by the crowd. I looked around for familiar knees, my mother's blue dress or her shoes, and I tilted my head upward to find a face I knew. But there was none. It was scary for a minute and then I just drifted with the crowd and when it stopped to look at something, I stopped too. I couldn't see much but there were some pens with ducks and rabbits and I could hear cows and sheep. Somewhere there was merry-go-round music. I had had two rides on that.

Finally I found myself marooned, like a tiny ship, wedged against a small building, caught between all those legs and a wooden wall and not too far above my head, a little roof. I could hear a man shouting and people laughing. "Step right up, win the little lady a kewpie doll." There would be a thup, thup, thup and shouts or sometimes dead silence. It was very hot in that little space and I ducked down and tried to crawl out but someone stepped on my hand and someone else stumbled over me until finally a big man, a funny smelling man, of peppermint and Bay Rum after-shave and tobacco and sweat, picked me up and called out to the crowd. "Anyone missing this little girl—she needs her mama." No one claimed me but a policeman came and carried me to another little building and set me on a high bench and asked me a lot of questions.

"Can you tell me your name?" Well of course I could, silly man. And that I lived in Mound City and my daddy's name was Denny and my mother was Minnie and we lived in the parsonage and had a dog named Buster and I had a big sister and a baby brother and please and thank you, I would like to go now. My mother would be worried.

"Don't you worry little lady, your mother will be here to get you any minute. How would you like an ice cream cone?"

I would like an ice cream cone very very much; ice cream was a rare treat in my young life. And I was quite enjoying the attention of several policemen gathered around me laughing and asking questions about Mound City and exclaiming "You don't say" when I mentioned our wooden sidewalks and Mrs. Kosel and my friends the Kolodzie brothers and Sonny Larsen and Noste's store and the Mercantile. I told them about my father's office that was in the jail and about our big white schoolhouse that my sister got to go to and about Deibert's pond and that my mother made doughnuts every Saturday. I told them everything I knew and they kept laughing and asking me more questions and I found the whole thing quite enjoyable,. especially after my second ice cream cone, which wasn't a cone at all like I was used to but more like a waffle sandwich with ice cream. Very good.

And then there was my father, his straw hat pushed way back on his head and a worried look on his face until he saw me. Then a whole lot of expressions crossed his face. He was happy and relieved and annoyed too—poor Mother was worried sick, the baby was tired and cranky and my sister didn't particularly like this dirty place. I think right then and there he decided the State Fair might be educational, maybe too educational, and it was no place for a family with three little kids and only two parents to look after them. He thanked the policemen, laughed with them at their accounts of my storytelling and lifted me down, took my hand firmly and instructed that if we should be separated even for a minute, to just stand still so he could find me. Frankly, I couldn't see what all the fuss was about. I had had a perfectly fine time, and was quite sure that I could take care of myself in any emergency.

I know it was a great relief to my parents when we arrived at Uncle Ernest's house in Leola. It was a big yellow three story building with dark wood inside and shades pulled against the sun. My cousin Buddy and I got to play hospital in the family car, a handsome big sedan that was parked beside the house. We picked peas for pills and used a funnel to listen to each other's hearts. After supper my mother didn't have to ask me twice to get ready for bed, I was asleep almost before I managed to get my shoes off. I dreamed of policemen and when I woke I could smell bacon and coffee and hear my mother and father and I knew Aunt Ella would be smiling gently and Uncle Ernest would look cross but he wasn't.

Hot Day in Mound City

2

THE CLOUDLESS SKY promised no relief. Looking toward the sun, we saw only shimmer—luminous, metallic shimmer. Our whole world was faded and dry. Heat soaked the moisture from our skin and hair. Tired old buildings, house, shed, outhouse, silvering in the prairie sun, seemed brittle and smelled of dust and dry rot. Our bodies were parched; we smelled of withering grass and the hard moistureless ground where we lay in the dust in a thin band of shade on the north side of the house, too hot to play, too hot to read, too hot even to talk. Dried grass and weeds poked us. A film of dust covered us. We closed our eyes against the glare. Only the occasional whir of grasshopper wings, the parched soughing of the ever present wind, now slowed to a whisper, reminded us of a living world.

Some signal, unspoken, passed between us, and my sister and I rose together to cross the yard, pull up the door to the fruit cellar and plunge into its murky depths. We hated the fruit cellar. Although it was twenty degrees cooler thạn outside, we braved its cobwebbed dimness only when ordered, or when we were desperate for some of its contents.

We emerged with a watermelon and a muskmelon. Cantaloupe was a word we didn't know. "Mushmelon" was the accepted name in our parts, but our parents insisted on the "k".

With a knife hanging by a string from a nail just up under the heavy slanted door, we opened a green globe. Its rind parted with a satisfactory crack. We hacked it into fair-sized pieces and then sliced into the golden muskmelon. My sister, the neat one, remembered to wipe the knife on a rag that shared nail space with it. I would have used my overalls.

We helped ourselves to the juicy treats, our throats grateful for their baths. Restored by the moisture and the sweetness, we talked and laughed quietly. Pauline, my friend, danced down the path to the outhouse doing her imitation of the turkey trot.

My mother came out of the house to sit on the steps, wiping her face and neck on her apron and fanning herself with it. She was pale in the heat. She sat with her housedress pulled above her knees, spread to let the air touch her skin underneath. Her dark hair was lank with sweat. Still the thought came to me, she is pretty. My mother is pretty. She smiled and accepted a bite of watermelon from my sister.

Inside, my baby brother lay sleeping in front of the screen door, his head pillowed on Buster's flank. The kitchen coal fire was out and would not be rebuilt that day. Anything that hadn't been cooked by now, wouldn't be. Water in the stove reservoir would stay warm enough to wash dishes and for spit baths.

The afternoon wore on. Twice we took turns pumping water over each other's heads and feet, taking care as we had been taught, not to let the soiled water run back into the well to foul our drinking water or spoil the pail of food—milk, butter and yesterday's roast beef—that hung in the water to stay cool.

Jack sat quietly in the shade with us, eating his share of melon, listening to our chatter. Almost always silent, he watched us with cool gray eyes. Only when one of our jokes struck him funny, would he make a sound. Then a rollicking, welling chuckle emerged from his serious little self. His delight was our ultimate accolade. Today it was too hot to laugh.

Finally, my father walked around the house, crunching on the gravel path, his suit coat and tie slung over his shoulder. He went to the well and pumped himself a tin cup of cool water and carried one to my mother.

Pauline slipped away home. The baby staggered out to Mother, his black hair wet and curly, diaper sagging. For a long time, we all sat quietly, waiting for evening's shadow.

"Martin says we are due for a thunderstorm," my dad murmured. He and Mother, my sister and I, exchanged glances, tremulous with hope.

Flying with Aunt Sis

A TRAIN WHISTLE'S MOURNFUL HOOTING across the prairie was both the lonesomest sound in the world and the most exciting. It evoked dreams of rushing through the landscape, passing the fields of wheat and corn to the edge of lakes, through giant mountain crags and across wondrous bridges that swayed in the wind. I imagined shining cities, verdant forests and valleys so green they would never turn to autumn gold or winter's dour gray. I wanted to go.

When my Aunt Sis came to visit from Minneapolis and brought our cousin Mary Margaret, her niece, she also brought with her a multitude of city ways. Nice little girls did not run around shirtless with only their overall straps to hide bony little chests. They didn't spend day after long summer day in the hot sun with no hat to protect them. She did not approve of brown little girls. Nor of scabby knees or callused feet from going barefoot every day but Sunday.

Where *she* came from, Aunt Sis never tired of saying,

mothers and their little girls dressed up each afternoon in their second best dresses, with ankle socks which had a bit of lace at the top, shiny Mary Janes, and a ribbon in their hair. My mother sighed deeply and was very busy during these exhortations, pretending not to hear. But as she told my father, "If Sis had to raise four kids and haul water from a pump to wash their dirty feet every evening, she'd put them up for adoption." Dad had to agree but he asked us all to be patient when she attacked our sun-browned faces with cucumbers to return them to their winter white and a new softness. It was a waste Mother thought, better to eat them in sandwiches or put them in jars with brine and dill.

Aunt Sis scared us more than a little, but when the idea arose to send us to Minneapolis with her on "The Flyer," I for one couldn't help being enthusiastic. To all questions whether I could promise to behave myself like a little lady, keep my voice down, my socks up and my nose clean, I insisted "yes." Mother was dubious but the thought of a few weeks with only two children, my younger brothers, swayed her. I think she laid a heavy load of responsibility on my sister who was not only a little older but much more civilized, probably a likelier human being in Aunt Sis's mind. She was also smarter and more reluctant to go, but she gave in.

Dad thought it would be very educational for us and a chance to get to know our Irish relatives a little better. He felt we had plenty of opportunity for learning from the German side of the family although he was very fond of them all, even my grandfather who didn't speak to him for two years after he married my mother. Dad instructed us about the train. The Flyer, he said, could not stop in every little town like Selby where we must go to board, but we would have to stand close to the rails and an arm would reach down and hoist us up and the conductor would grab us and pull us in. Even that didn't dampen my ardor for the trip.

We were scrubbed to a fare thee well, dressed in our best and hurried to Selby to board the train which "did too stop, Daddy," but not for long. A kiss, a hug and remonstrations to behave that echoed down the track as we pulled out of the station and we were off, alone with Aunt Sis. With our cousin Mary Margaret too, of course, who despite her city ways, we liked quite a lot. Her skin was pinkly white and she didn't own any overalls so I guess she and Aunt Sis were better companions.

Ah, but the thrill of that ride. The train mournfully wailed its way through crossings and little towns, slowing just long enough to pick up passengers and packages. I waved vigorously to the local bystanders who were always there to lift their caps and wave and smile. How lucky I felt to be inside, riding like a queen. I knew what it was like to be one of them, standing enviously by the tracks, feeling lonesome and left out. A freight train went through my grandparents' hometown, and it was one of the magnets that made me love to visit them. Once I was there to proudly wave good-bye to my uncle who was taking a load of cattle to Minneapolis. Oh, lucky uncle, he got to ride in the caboose. And my grandfather was there to shake his hand roughly and issue instructions in a loud voice as the train pulled out, huffed and hooted its way into the prairie.

The railroad engineers and firemen were never too busy to wave and smile at gazers, the brakeman would lift his striped cap as he patrolled the track while the cattle were loaded. All this romance, this pageantry, in a tiny prairie town with barely two hundred souls—and all for me I was sure. Busy men, bawling cattle, the golden river of grain being loaded, theater without walls.

It was a magic ride on that train to Minneapolis, watching the landscape turn greener, more treed, seeing tiny houses and barns turn regular size, counting the birds lined up on telephone wires. My aunt removed herself from us just far enough so she had a bit of privacy but within monitoring range so that our country ways would not be allowed to show too much. Finally, she made her way down the aisle to us to say it was time for dinner, not supper, dinner.

What could be more exciting. I was awed when we entered the dining car with its white linen-covered tables and the shining black faces of the waiters in starchy white jackets. They were jovial and pleasant and my aunt was probably less than approving of the friendliness of our conversation. One was to be polite, but cool, to "servants" and that is what she considered them. But despite the glint in her eye and her sharp tongue, she had a ready if equally sharp wit and we loved her, sometimes.

In the dining car confronted with a menu printed on heavy paper, I couldn't make a decision. The cheese sandwich and dish of peas that Aunt Sis suggested wouldn't do. But what were these glamorous foods, filet mignon, for example—which I of course pronounced underlining the final letter in filet and the hard "g" in mignon? I don't remember what I ordered as a main course and I am sure I was too excited to eat it all. But, it was dessert that got me into real trouble.

I had never seen the word frappé, had no idea what it was nor how to pronounce it. It was a delightful combination of ice cream, fruit and whipped cream, Aunt Sis educated me, and it was not a frap or a frappie. While I waited for the waiter to bring mine I practiced pronouncing it until my sister and cousin Mary Margaret threatened mayhem. It was deliciously pink and fruity and I was savoring every bite, stretching my delight, interminably I suppose, when the two girls asked to be excused and jumped up to leave the table. Torn between the frappé and being left out, I jumped up too, grabbed the fluted glass and to my dear aunt's horror, tipped it to my lips.

Banished to the top bunk immediately after that fiasco, I lay waiting for my sister listening to the lonesome whistle as the train sped into the dark. She forgot her embarrassment at my behavior long enough to giggle as we managed to pull off our clothes and stow them in the little hammock and tug on our pajamas and robes in the claustrophobic confinement of our upper berth. Forgetting to summon the porter and his little ladder, I slid down and made my unsteady way to the restroom clutching my toothbrush. People politely ignored nightclothes and each one gave the other all the room possible to pass in the aisle. Actually, train travel brought out the best in most people, even me. There was something friendly, yet just a wee bit formal, different from home, that made me try to watch my p's and q's. But, I certainly allowed nothing to spoil my pleasure in that ride across the prairie at top speed, coal smoke blowing in the wind.

Our arrival at the railroad station in Minneapolis was as exciting as the trip, and I gazed open-mouthed in amazement at red caps hustling loaded luggage carts, streams of people, honking taxis—I was in no hurry to leave. But everyone else was, especially Aunt Sis, and I was dragged protesting all the way to a taxi and a long summer of city life, interesting but, I thought, very confining.

Visiting the City

A TRIP TO MINNEAPOLIS was such an exciting thing that although I missed my parents and the freedom of my prairie life, I cherished each day. Wherever I turned there were new sights and sounds and smells. It was a noisy world with clanging streetcars, newsboys calling out headlines and automobiles honking as they whizzed by. The rag and bottle man's plaintive cry "Any old rags, bo-o-otles, old bones" sent me rushing to the curb to watch his procession down the street, the old wagon creaking, and his bony horse with the straw hat snuffling and farting along.

Evenings the popcorn wagon made its way up and down the street, its little whistle familiar to all, the glowing gas burner that popped the corn smelling the air. It was so exciting I didn't even require the popcorn to make me happy.

My big boy cousins, young men actually, were kind and funny, and I loved it when Ray swung me around and threatened to eat my eye for a grape although I screeched in mock horror and we all begged Les Junior to "Play it again, play it again" when he sat down to the piano to murder *The Twelfth Street Rag*. Evenings we played across the street on the lawn of the Minneapolis Art Institute chasing the squirrels and I sneaked bits of food to them despite my aunts' warning that they would get into their attic if we encouraged them. Uncle Lester liked his evenings in the living room quiet so he could listen to the scratchy radio through his earphones and once the dishes were done and the family busy elsewhere Aunt Margaret enjoyed a quiet cup of tea alone or with Aunt Sis at her dining table.

I found it fascinating to live with a toilet right in the house and a built-in bathtub and sink with running water. It seemed to me people spent an awful lot of time in that room and there was a great deal of interest in the natural functions of one's body. I had never heard of constipation unless one were sick and then a hated but hearty dose of castor oil was in order. My mother never questioned me anxiously about my "regularity" and I was not bribed with sweets to swallow a physic except when I was suffering chills and fever and then I had no choice.

Baths at our house were weekly affairs and we washed our feet in the shed before bedtime in summer. In the city it was so simple to turn the faucet and get a gush of hot water, I found myself looking for opportunities to bathe. With eight of us and one tub, those opportunities came less frequently than I hoped.

My Aunt May, who lived in St. Paul, owned a tearoom downtown in the Bremer Arcade, The Millcrest was its name. To us it seemed the grandest place and to ride in her car all the way across the bridge on the Mississippi River and have lunch there was a treat. The car had a history of its own. It had been found for her, second hand, by a second cousin's husband who was in the garage business. I can't remember the make, but it was a fancy car with thick leather seats, a glass window between front and back because it supposedly had been driven by a chauffeur, and it had a tricky well in its floor, where the former owner had kept hidden his bootleg liquor. That was how he earned such luxuries, but alas, apparently the Feds had gotten him and he languished in jail while we rode around the city in his car.

The Millcrest, which the family called "the shop," had started life as a soda fountain. And my aunt loved to tell how she and her erstwhile partner had gone off to Chicago to buy the necessary appointments. They had dressed in all the finery they could muster, a dear friend who had a tailoring business had made for Aunt May a dove gray suit with a very tight skirt, narrow at the hem, so that walking was a jiggly and apparently enticing art. At the supplier's they insisted on a marble soda fountain, only French marble would do. May had read somewhere that French marble was the very latest thing and it must be exactly the color of her dove gray suit. Apparently they smiled and batted their lashes sufficiently to get invited to lunch and for the business's owner to overlook their lack of financial resources, and they went home assured that all of the necessary equipment would arrive in time for their scheduled grand opening and they could pay as they went.

Among the joys of city visiting were movies—always preceded by variety acts. It was the heyday of vaudeville and comedians including couples similar to George Burns and Gracie Allen, sometimes with their little children, were often on the bill. As I remember, a famous singer, Mitzi someone, sang "Give me a little kiss, now will ya, huh? And I'll give it right back to you." I thought that was the cleverest collection of words I had ever heard or would ever hear. It made me laugh all over and we sang it to one another constantly, my cousin, my sister and I, mimicking Miss Mitzi. We made the aunts laugh too, and even Uncle Lester smiled at us—especially at my sister and me. I don't think he thought it was appropriate material for his daughter.

But the most thrilling thing was the organ which rose out of a pit to its place on the stage, its gold pipes gleaming in the flashes of red and amber and blue from revolving spotlights. It was, as a song went that the organist played, "simply gorgeous." Actually the movies, silent of course, were just a little icing on the cake after all these wonderful surprises, and I hated to leave the theater when the lights came up. Sometimes I prevailed upon whatever adult was in charge to stay, "just a little while" so we could watch the organ rise again and the next acts start.

And then we got to go to the circus—Ringling Brothers Barnum and Bailey—in a huge tent that smelled of popcorn, dust and elephant dung. Marvel succeeded marvel, lions and tigers and elephants, horses with scantily clad girls riding bareback, standing up! And clowns! And the trapeze artists that frightened me so I could hardly watch them swing through the air and fly free and catch one another. Every time one of them let go, my heart would plummet, but I always peeked out of my almost closed lids to see them land safely. We ate prodigiously of cotton candy and ice cream and peanuts which we shared with the elephants when we toured the grounds. I fear we gawked mercilessly at the fat lady, the jungle boy and the half-woman half-snake. It broke my heart that the adults were anxious to leave. They had had enough of the dirt and the heat, and there was too little magic left for them to want to linger longer.

After these expeditions, we went to the shop for supper and were allowed to choose anything we wanted to eat: chicken, roast beef, lamb stew (I never chose that) and any exotic dessert that was on the menu. It was hard—fried chicken wasn't the problem, it was the dessert—pie of every kind, cake—coconut, chocolate or lemon, peach cobbler, apricot meringue and of course orange sherbet. I could never get enough orange sherbet and once one of the waitresses taught me to slather some hot fudge on it—well, all of the other choices fell away. But good Aunt May, she always sent us off with a care package, plenty of sweets for an army.

I was impressed with the city, with street cars and the bustle and traffic and of course the tall buildings. The tallest ones in Mound city were two story—except the courthouse. It seemed enormous to me and may have had a third story. The only other tall structures were silos to be found on farms and grain elevators which stood beside the railroad tracks in towns lucky enough to have railroad tracks. Mound City did not although we kept mounting campaigns to get a spur to come to our town. My friends and I used to stand beside the highway and chant—
"Can we win it? Well I guess.
Mound City Railroad, yes, yes, yes!"
My Uncle Chris was a figure of some mystery to me. He was a supervisor of heating and plumbing in Minneapolis's tallest building, the Foshay Tower, I think was its name. When my parents came to take us home, at my father's suggestion, as a special treat and an educational opportunity besides, he agreed to take us all to the top of the tower. The elevator ride was a dizzying experience, I couldn't believe it could possibly know how to stop at the very top and I worried that we might explode through the roof and go soaring into the atmosphere leaving my insides behind.

I vaguely remember the view, the jumble of the city at our feet, cars the size of toys whizzing through the streets. A bit farther out there were emerald lawns and elm trees, all of which looked like the toy pieces of a board game. The Mississippi River glinted through the trees and as far as the eye could see, there was the blue of lakes and beyond them fields and a straggle of houses. My father instructed us where to look and explained what we were seeing. I tried to pay attention but mostly I studied Uncle Chris.

I thought of him as a big man, very big. But reason and family photos tell me he was average size, only slightly taller than my father and my Uncle Jim. He wasn't like either of them.

Dad was the baby brother, the smart one, and a lovable, interesting fellow, his siblings agreed, who was a whiz at some things, could charm an audience or an individual but would never be worth a cent. He just didn't seem to understand about money, or care much, although he did like to spend it. His sisters worried that he would spend a lot of time in purgatory since he had left the Catholic faith, but he would eventually get to heaven they believed, he was such a good man.

Uncle Jim was a roly-poly red faced Irishman who said "dese, dose and dem." Even then I knew when he had been drinking more than he ought for it showed. It made him heartier than usual, louder and more ashes dripped from his hand rolled cigarettes, faster than ever. I knew he liked me. He called me girlie and squeezed my hand and rubbed his whiskery face against mine. My mother bridled. I liked him a lot and the quarters he slipped into my hand now and then.

Uncle Chris on the other hand, was silent. As he gazed out at the landscape in his fine suit and polished shoes, his shock of black hair which rose in a crest from his forehead, and his big nose, a little pointed upward at the tip, blocked my view of the cloudless August sky. I don't remember that he said a word. I thought his attitude was, here it is, my domain, all mine. I'm giving you a peek. He made me feel humble and out of place although he probably didn't mean to.

Uncle Jim was often around the house when my parents visited my aunts and my grandfather was there too. But we went to visit Uncle Chris and his family in their apartment. My Aunt Mae Grace fussed over us loudly and allowed us to pet her ugly, smelly old bulldog. She loved him deeply and let him sleep on her fur coat. When you touched him, he snuffled and slobbered but he rarely bothered to get to his feet. Uncle Chris was a silent presence.

My cousins, both young men then, that I remember in knickers, teased us a bit and smiled and left. Aunt Mae Grace opened her favorite, a can of greengage plums and put out a plate of cookies, Mary Annes, they were called, hard and tasteless with a brittle crust of white sugary frosting.

"Come on, you little Protestant dogs, eat up now and don't forget to thank Jesus for his favor." She laughed and hugged us and left us to eat.

She talked exhaustively about the church and the nuns and the priest, she called him Father, no other name to differentiate him from any other father, and about mutual friends, the Connoly girls. Her hair was always freshly dyed a glowing strawberry red and was tightly curled. We'd been told she wound it up on kid curlers every night. Forewarned that she was to have company, she was fussily dressed in drapey silk or satin with lots of gold chains and high-heeled slippers that would have done credit to a ball gown and crippled her feet.

Sometimes she bridled and arched and touched Uncle

Chris, teasing him and telling us little stories about him. It made me feel a little sorry for her and I loved her more than usual for it didn't seem to me he even heard her. His eyes rarely moved and his face remained impassive. Unless you talked baseball. Then he came alive and described plays, runs batted in, high flies, catches that did a player proud and errors that shamed another. He rattled off statistics and rose from his chair to pace nervously as he talked. You could see his arms tense and his hands grip the bat that wasn't there. I knew that's what he had always wanted to be. It made me sad for both of them because instead he ended up married, with a baby, trapped in the Foshay Tower.

Oh those were lovely days, riding streetcars, looking anxiously for our stop, tripping through department stores and peering into the windows of restaurants, barber shops, beauty salons. Poor Aunt Sis was mortified to be associated with this curious child of few manners who asked people embarrassing questions like, "Why do you cover him up with that towel?" to the neighborhood barber at whom I had been staring through the open door. But when I boldly asked the conductor if I could ring the bell on the street-car, that was too much. He graciously allowed me to clang at every stop until we got off, several blocks before we needed to.

Even more wonderful than matinees and circuses were those times I thought of as Lady Sundays. Mass was over, Sunday dinner picked to the bone, dishes washed and the kitchen clean. The menfolk had gone off to their own pursuits, a long comfortable nap for Uncle Les and young men's adventures for my cousins Ray and Lester. Now the aunts, Margaret, May and Sis and maybe Mae Grace, and their friends Nell and Mary and cousin Anne gathered in the living room or on the front porch. Gone were the corsets and high heels of the earlier day, and they sat slouched comfortably in kimonos, stockings rolled to the knees, imparting a heady fragrance of talcum powder, lotion and flesh.

They barely noticed our presence, for my sister and cousin enjoyed these times as much as I. We watched the women page through fashion magazines commenting on the latest styles and beauty secrets. They sipped tea or later in the day, a highball, told the latest Pat and Mike stories and massaged their skin with oil, peered for new wrinkles, blackheads or unwanted hairs. They talked comfortably about clothes, men, whether to dye their hair, if so, what color, and they advised each other frankly. "No, no, not blonde for you, May, Margaret, yes, and red for Sis, but you have to keep that black hair. Just touch it up."

They read tea leaves and horoscopes and made little jokes, a few of which were too obscure for me to understand. They read our tea leaves too and consulted the stars for the three of us. We learned whether we would marry, at what age, what our worst faults were, what areas of the body would cause us concern throughout our lifetime and whether we would live good long lives. Of course we would, but we were warned that we must pass through troublesome times, beware of certain men and drink lots of water.

The kimonos would gape and breasts would emerge from the folds, knees would peek from beneath the skirts. I was totally conscious of womanhood, of feminine presence. I liked their smells, their laughter, the cigarettes that dangled from their lips as they turned the pages of a magazine and soaked their fingers as part of a manicure. And I loved the jokes. Once Mary, leafing through a magazine, held up an ad for a breast reducer which showed bulbous, fatty breasts changed into pert youthful ones. Mary flipped up her huge pendulous breasts and said, "Then what would I do, toss them over my shoulder?" The women shared a laugh, and I collapsed under the table hysterical at my mental image of Mary with big long breasts like stockings stuffed with fat legs thrown over her shoulder.

Those afternoons linger in my memory. I tried but couldn't quite imagine my mother in dishabille, part of them, smoke drifting to the ceiling, cracker crumbs and bits of cheese spilled on the tablecloth, faces cracking under the beauty masks, almond shaped nails, and jokes, mostly about men, some of which I didn't understand but recognized somehow as womanly wisdom. There were sighs and groans at the thought of squeezing back into clothes and shoes to take the streetcar home. Aunt Margaret began to worry about what to feed everyone for supper, and we could hear stirrings in the upstairs where Uncle Les had been resting. The women pulled on their clothes and made the final laughing comments about spending a day at O'Reilly's funeral parlor for a good make-over, kissed the air about each other's heads and hurried off toward home or the kitchen. It wasn't Monday yet, but Sunday was over.

Wonderful as they were, before long I was ready to abandon the pleasures of the city. I wanted to go home to my mother and father. I wanted to be where I could ask questions and no one cared. I wanted to stop wearing shoes and socks and dresses every single day. Oh, to be back in my beloved overalls, barefoot, squinching my feet in the warm dust, pumping water over each other's heads on a hot day. I wanted my mother's comfortable presence and her home cooking and my dad's voice telling stories and singing songs.

At night I read over his letters—printed large so I could make them out—his version of fairy stories, about how the sidewalk rolled up at night in sorrow because we weren't there, and the gophers came right up to the house to see why we hadn't been out in the pasture and the bluebells only bloomed on Sunday so the church could have a bouquet, but the rest of the week, they drooped, moping in our absence. Even the meadow larks stopped singing!

It was time to go home. How I loved it—it looked so beautiful, that old brown house and the Model T and the town in the moonlight waiting for me to visit every place, every house and building and tell about my adventures in Minneapolis and hear how many gophers Willis caught and who got ducked in the pond and who won the last game of Run Sheep Run. Was anyone sick? Were there new babies, calves, dogs, kittens? Was Mr. Hegel's leg bothering him, or the judge's lumbago? I couldn't sleep, I knew I wouldn't sleep, but the morning sun woke me, and Mother didn't even try to restrain me. I went out to reclaim my place. I was home, I wanted everyone to know.

Harvest Time

⤳

THERE WAS A CERTAIN SMELL to harvest, the dry smell of seed and chaff mixed with the aroma of horse sweat and manure and the acrid fumes of the threshing machine. I was allowed to ride in the wagon called a header box where the seeds, the heads, landed after the stalks of grain were threshed. I loved the hot sunshine, the heady talk of the Hofer sisters as they worked, their laughter and teasing underlined by the deep voices of their brothers. Harvest was a family affair and I was included because when Martha Hofer, our hired girl, went home to help with the harvest, she took me with her to lighten my mother's load.

It was a treat for me to be the only child among so many cheerful, adoring adults. When I tired of the long hours in the field, I swatted flies in the dairy for five cents for every hundred corpses and read the weekly newspaper to Papa Hofer, who was blind. He always said the only time he really knew what was going on was when I was there. I faithfully read who had stopped for dinner with whom, named the guests at local church bazaars and dinners, itemized the calendars of the Ladies Aid Societies and the Oddfellows Lodge. And I left out not a single obituary, no advertisement for feed and seed sales.

I helped Mrs. Hofer carry the noon dinners to the field. We carried sacks of fried chicken and "butter bread," garden tomatoes, ginger cookies and pails of lemonade, then joined the family to picnic in the shade of the wagons.

Sometimes I would be invited to drive the horses, always being warned to keep straight so the wheat would land where it should in the wagon. We sucked on peppermints and lemon drops to keep the saliva flowing and stopped now and then for long drinks of water from jugs kept cool by their wrappings of wet gunny sacks. Field work went on into twilight of the long hot late summer days and then there were still chores to be done. The livestock must be fed, eggs gathered and the last preparations made for the hearty supper everyone would eat. Bursting with pot roast and gravy and pie we all finally staggered wearily off to bed.

I was sent to wash my dusty feet and hands and rinse my sunburned face at the backyard pump before I climbed onto the featherbed in the main house. Meals and all other activities took place in the summer kitchen, a free standing, huge, screened room with the dairy attached but we slept in the big two-storied main house. Many times I woke to find the family long gone and I whiled away the morning until time to carry dinner to the field. One of my favorite pastimes, when I tired of reading and swatting flies, was to bathe the ducklings in the horse tank. They squawked long and loud at my ministrations to the great entertainment of the Hofers when their mother told them the story at supper time.

Saturday nights were a bustle of activity. Field work

stopped a bit early, everyone gulped a cold supper of ham and deviled eggs and took turns bathing in the horse tank. Male eyes were averted while the women sloshed and rinsed and females gave the same consideration to the men. The tank was emptied and rinsed and clean water provided for the livestock. In the big house bedrooms the girls dressed in their best, carefully powdered their sun-reddened faces, streaked on pale pink lipstick and we all headed to town in the Model T. All of us except Mr. and Mrs. Hofer.

But first came the ceremony of paying each of the sons and daughters their week's wages. Like children, these huge, hearty men and women lined up before their blind father and accepted silver dollars he doled out for their hard work. He counted them carefully, listening with satisfaction to the heavy clink of coins one against another. When it came my turn, he pressed a fifty cent piece into my hand. I was rich beyond my dreams.

In town, I was sworn to silence and the "boys" took off to the poolroom for a beer and a game or two of pool. Their sisters and I made the rounds of the stores to look at yard goods and trimmings and buy supplies for the next week. Except for the youngest. She met a forbidden admirer in secret. Papa did not approve of these Saturday night pleasures nor of the young man courting his daughter. To insure my silence, I was taken to the candy store and treated to a huge selection of penny candy, a bag of lemon drops, a box of chocolates and plenty of peppermint ribbon candy to last all week. My supply was big enough to share, and the sister of the secret lover, brave Anita, especially enjoyed the treats. She always laughingly insisted her generous bites were necessary to even off the chunk of ribbon candy I was eating.

When we got home Saturday night, our wheels sounding a warning on the gravel road, Papa came to the door and "watched" silently as the bags and boxes of groceries and feed were unloaded. The few small packages of personal purchases were spirited to the girls' bedrooms by one of them while the others chattered bustling about the kitchen setting out cookies and making sandwiches for a before-bed snack. Satisfied that his flock was home, safe and sober, the boys smelling of freshly chewed spearmint gum, Papa joined Mrs. Hofer in bed where she was trying to recharge herself for another day.

Sunday, usually a strictly observed day of rest, only differed from the other days during harvest season by Bible study and prayers. Papa couldn't see to read but he must have known every page of the Bible by heart and he prayed at great length. I could see his sons pursing their lips and silently shuffling their feet in exasperation while the girls peered up from beneath their bowed heads. One of them always winked at the others, setting off paroxysms of silent, suppressed laughter.

Finally the religious observances were done and we headed gratefully to the barns to harness the teams and start the threshing machine. Harvest was almost over, now the crops would be sold, and preparations begun for winter. I would go home to start school and Martha would bid her family a tearful good-bye. I was sad too, but rich; my fifty cent pieces and fly swatting nickels carefully hoarded for treats to brighten the long winter. And I knew that the sisters, one by one, would show up at our house for a little visit, a vacation from the labor and isolation of the big farm. And I would hear their secrets again, follow their romances, and feast on candy treats to insure my silence while I waited for the next harvest.

Autumn

❧

BOOKS WERE A LARGE PART of our lives. Once I mastered the essentials of reading, I spent happy hours in every season reading fairy tales, fables, kids' books, adult books, magazines and newspapers, anything I could put my hands on. And through reading I formed perceptions of faraway places.

Autumn in other places, I learned, was marked by clear, winey days, brightly colored leaves which dropped to the ground and covered old grass. I could smell the tangy smoke of bonfires when the raked up heaps of gold and red were fed to the flames. But I never understood why anyone would want to do away with such beauty as my books described when they spoke of autumn.

Our autumns on the prairie were different. There were too few trees to shed ground covers of amber and scarlet. Those there were seemed to simply yellow and grow sere, finally turning black against the winter sky. But we watched the Russian thistles dry and turn brittle until one day a wind swept them from their stems into heaps against fences and buildings. Now they became truly tumbling weeds, the name by which they were known in other places, rolling across the prairie, roads, and vacant lots until some impediment stopped them.

A prairie bonfire in autumn was not of autumn leaves but of piles and piles of Russian thistles, pulled from fences, and pitch forked from their resting places against houses and barns. The smell of that smoke, pungent enough to bring tears, spelled autumn to us.

Now we began earnest preparations for winter. The shelves of root cellars and pantries were lined with jars and jars of vegetables and fruit, heavy with a winter's supply of jam and sauce and green beans and peas and pickles. Crocks of sauerkraut fermented odiferously and eggs and green tomatoes were buried in boxes of oats and stored in the fruit cellar.

The minute my mother was satisfied that there was food a plenty to see us through the cold months and jelly and jam and fruit to break the monotony of winter meals, she turned her thoughts to the second of the great cleaning orgies that took place each year. Summer dust and dirt must be removed to be replaced by the lingering smell of Fels Naptha soap and moth balls.

Again every exposed inch of floor and wall had to be scrubbed and carpets and matresses turned out to be sunned and beaten into cleanliness. Summer cretonnes were removed from windows, pillows, sofas and chairs to be washed and ironed and stored away for the next spring. Winter decorations were returned to their places of honor; bouquets of dried flowers and grasses, and freshly ironed embroidered table scarves adorned the living room.

Summer quilts were washed and folded with sprigs of lavender or potpourri of a few scarce rose petals, cloves, and cinnamon sticks and squirreled away in trunks and closets. Out came winter blankets and quilts, redolent of moth balls to be hung on the line to air. Airing was only partially successful in removing the smells and far into winter, one could pull the covers overhead and inhale along with the body smell of healthy children only bathed weekly and bedding washed clean even less often, the faint pungent remnants of last summer's moth balls.

Now too, our winter clothes, heavy coats and jackets, mufflers and mittens were brought forth from the boxes where they had been entombed for the summer. Overshoes were rescued from summer storage in the coal shed and Mother rested from her labors of housecleanig by inspecting the long black stockings, the voluminous black bloomers and despised long underwear into which we would be buttoned and gartered for another long winter.

There was always a good deal of tongue clicking and head shaking over how much all of us had grown.

"Let's see now," Mother would worry aloud, "if Elizabeth has to have Kathleen's coat, I wonder if I could make her one out of that coat Aunt May sent. " Unfortunately, my feet always ran to size so overshoes could never be passed on to me. New ones when they were purchased had to be sexless so that my sister's went to Jack, the older of my two younger brothers. At least one mitten always turned up missing and a new pair had to be purchased or solicited from Grandma Kusler, the family knitter.

All mittens, old and new, were pinned to a sturdy cord that was often made of braided multicolor odds and ends of yarn. These cords were sewed or pinned to the inside collars of our coats and passed through the sleeves. There was no good excuse for losing a mitten. And our mothers frowned on the common practice among children of using the back of a mittened hand as a handkerchief on cold days.

For several Saturdays, my father was occupied shoveling a smelly mixture of dirt and manure around the inadequate foundation of our house. This was to keep the winter winds from freezing the floors. Now too, the garden was prepared for winter and storm windows came out to replace summer's screens and storm doors took the place of screen doors at both entrances to the house. The coal man brought wagon loads of coal to be dumped in the shed. My sister and I eyed this development with dismay. Any day now we would be expected to fill an extra tub with coal and haul it on the wagon to the kitchen door. A job we did not fancy.

My mother eyed all of these preparations for winter with great satisfaction and one night we heard her say, "Den, I think it's time to bring in the stove." Winter was at hand, we knew.

With the help of neighbors, the freshly blacked base burner was carried in to the front room and set on its asbestos pad. The chrome gleamed and the black belly shone spotless. Chimney pipes were fitted together all the way through the upstairs and out the chimney vent. "Can we have a fire," we begged, "can we?"

"Maybe tomorrow," Mother said, enjoying, wanting to enjoy just a few more hours, the clean shine of polished stove, with no coal dust, no clinkers and no soot.

It seemed to us that installing the stove for winter was a signal heralding the last gasp of summer, Indian summer, we called it. For the day after that event inevitably turned hot and the stove could not be lit, our mother informed us with relief.

Autumn was school and work and bonfires and preparation for the prairie winter. If it lacked the color of autumns in other places, it had a beauty of its own. The sun shone, thinly perhaps, and the air was clean and sharp. We watched the stubbled wheat turn to silver and the haystacks lose their last touch of green to turn pale gold. Birds etched the autumn sky with black and mice scurried to their hiding places with stores of seed for the long winter. We could see the horses putting on their shaggy winter coats.

Finally one morning our breath turned to smoke, the grass was brittle with frost and the last corn stalks bent and crumbled in the morning cold. When Mother sent us out to the root cellar for potatoes and squash for noon dinner, it was a comfort to see the bins and sacks and shelves of food to last the winter.

It was time for the first fire in the front room stove. We huddled in its heat to dress that morning and looked forward to our first night of cold weather. There would be hot cocoa for supper and maybe popcorn around the stove in the evening. We would miss the warm days and balmy nights of summer, but there was something enticing in the thought of evening games outside, buttoned against the chill of night air and then of that last hour before bed, sitting around the stove or playing and snacking at the round oak table in the kitchen, kettle steamimg on the cooking range, slabs of homemade bread and jam and cups of cocoa to see us off to bed and through the night.

Back to School

∾

THE AUTUMN PRAIRIE was faded gold interrupted by freshly plowed fields cleared of stubble and made ready for winter wheat or allowed to lie fallow to soak up the rain and snow that were to come. In unplowed pastures, cattle browsed and in farmyards pigs and chickens rooted in the last of summer's garden.

My sister and I went off to school no matter what the temperature in the finery our mother sat up late at night sewing for the coming season. Plaid wool perhaps for a dress made over from an aunt's; Mother's old brown suit recut and pieced to make a jumper for one and a jacket for another. Grandfathers and uncles contributed their discarded coats and trousers to be cut down for the boys, unless you were a farm boy and then you wore overalls. And many a town boy would gladly have traded his knickers for bibs and a pocket for every imaginable use.

No recognition of the common sense our mothers preached caused any little girl to set off for school in those first autumn days of golden sun and dry heat in our faded and outgrown vacation clothes. We stuffed our feet, callused from a barefoot summer, into shoes that must see us through the next year and robed ourselves in winter weights of wool to sit sweating and itchy in the stuffy schoolroom.

The smell of those rooms, mingled chalk and sweeping compound and milky little bodies that were bathed once a week and had clean clothes as often, was pungent. No matter how thoroughly cleaned and aired the school was in preparation for the new term, within an hour of our arrival the old smell was back, unmistakable, to grow stronger with each passing day.

In those warm early days of the school year, we drowsed through reading, writing and arithmetic lulled by the lazy buzz of captured flies, our eyelids heavy, our breaths slowing. What relief when the teacher announced recess and we could bolt for the play yard to quarrel over swings and teeter-totters. "I can pump higher than you can," we sang to each other and forgetting discomfort pushed ourselves to the top of the swing stands so that we could see over the iron bars, gleeful in our momentary freedom.

Recess over, our wise teacher led us in song or read to us from a story book that would accompany us through the year. Only when our spirits had subsided and our pumping blood calmed a bit were we asked to return to geography and spelling.

At noon the town kids walked home to dinner and glasses of milk and a doughnut or cookie from the ready supply most mothers kept on hand. The country kids ate at school, lunches they produced from bags they had tied to the bridle of the horses they rode bareback early every morning after chores were done on the farm. Not unusually, their lunches would be left-over pancakes from break-

fast smeared with molasses or sorghum syrup, or soda bis-
cuits with homemade jelly and a slice of home-cured ham.

Later, when winter set in in earnest, a mother or two,
with the help of a student who finished work quickly or was
being rewarded for exemplary conduct, would stir up a pot
of vegetable soup or escalloped potatoes in the basement
kitchen and we would all eat together, country kids and
town kids, big kids and little ones.

The school was a low white building with broad
wooden steps divided in half by a wide hall. On either side
of the hall was a large classroom with cloak rooms at the
front. On the right as you entered was the Big Room which
housed the fifth through eighth grades, and on the left,
the Little Room for first through fourth grades. There was
no kindergarten. At the back of the building, wooden stairs
led to the basement which housed the high school and the
kitchen. Behind it were the outhouses, two holers, one for
each room.

School hours were nine to four, but in the early fall,
light lingered long on the northern plains and we rushed
home to shed our scratchy clothes and don overalls for
outdoor play. We ran and tussled in the dusty vacant lot
next door working off the energy that accumulated in a
sedentary school day. We led one another on Trips through
Hades, our name for endurance contests when we ran blind-
folded through tangles of Russian thistles until any part of
our body that was bare was scraped and bleeding—the winner was the one who may have howled the loudest, but lasted
longest. We slept peacefully that night, ready for another day.

I see it now, my school, the water pail from which we
all drank, the coal stove in the center of the room (those
closest fried and those nearest the windows shivered) our
reading circle in the front, map cases on the walls, black-

boards, and in the back the sand table. I remember Miss Dynan's voice reading to us from *The Wizard of Oz*, the puppet shows we did, "Epaminandus, you ain't got the sense you were born with," the Latta book full of projects to do when lessons were finished, our rhythm band, poems we memorized, "The wind was a torrent of darkness," and recited for each other and for our parents on program nights. I remember sun and cloudless skies beckoning and the lonely sound of Canada geese honking overhead and blowing snow and the joy of being together, warm and safe.

I loved school.

Miss Dynan lives in my mind as the perfect teacher. When you thought of her you remembered her big-toothed smile, her wavy black hair and the genuine love she seemed to feel for every student and the work of teaching us. She was charged with energy and she charged us. Nothing was too difficult when you had Miss Dynan to inspire you. Over and over we were surprised to find we had just scaled heights, conquered difficult lessons without even knowing it. And she never scolded us, never slapped a hand or even sent us in blushing embarrassment to sit in the corner with another student who had shared our whispered conversation. Her only weapon was to look disappointed, as if our little failures hurt her far more than they hurt us. And we didn't want to hurt Miss Dynan.

There were other teachers I remember, although they weren't mine. There was one who taught the Big Room, I have lost her name, but she didn't look like a Mound City person. Her hair was smartly waved and curled but kept a measure of its natural buoyancy. She wore makeup and twirly skirts. Her features were sharp and it seemed to me her eyes were always looking at something far away, something I couldn't see. She often stood over the hot air register in the floor of the Big Room when we sang, letting her skirts blow about her legs, revealing more than we were used to, maybe more than she should have.

And there was Miss Macy. I think she may have taught in the new high school that was established in the basement of the school. She was old, very old, I thought, and wore rusty black dresses and tinted glasses. Her hair was white, her skin was wrinkled, but she was a friend. I liked Miss Macy, she came to our house for dinner sometimes and she was interesting to listen to, but best of all she listened to me. And once we shared the outhouse just like two equals, both of us struggling with out undergarments, reaching for suitable wiping material in the box of catalogue sheets and fruit wrappers. We walked back to the house together, Miss Macy's sensible shoes squeaking at every step, and took turns at the washbasin in the kitchen. I learned a lot from teachers, in school and out.

My first grade teacher was Miss Olson, Marguerite was her first name. I have a picture of her with her hair perfectly marcelled and wearing a feathery fur collar which must have been oh so soft, and maybe just a little tickley around her face. I was very impressed with Miss Olson. She was an entertainer and we spent our school days watching her and listening in delight as she recited poetry to us or told us pretty little stories. She seemed to agree that phonics and numbers were pretty difficult and got boring after a very short while, so she required very little of us in the way of attention to work. And we required very little of her.

The recitation we liked the best was the one about Bobby Shaftoe who went to sea, silver buckles on his knee. Poor Bobby Shaftoe, he came to a sad end. And as Miss Olson recited in dramatic voice, complete with gestures, his sad fate, she blew like the wind and made us feel the rising waters that were his end. We wept for him. Poor Bobby Shaftoe. Poor Miss Olson.

It became apparent to my father that I was not reading about the little red hen when asked to display my learning at the supper table. "Who will grind the wheat?" I said in my best inquisitorial manner. "I will," I declaimed for the little red hen. "And what is that word," my father asked, pointing.

"That one?" I questioned, hastily scanning the page for a clue. And when I began to recite the story from the beginning, following with my finger to the word he indicated, which I would not recognize but would know, for I knew the story letter perfect, he stopped me. In the days that followed there were conferences, Dad and Miss Olson, Dad and the school board, Dad and other parents and when it was determined that none of us could read, most could not even recognize letters or numbers, Miss Olson was banished.

Mrs. Groves came to take her place. We missed Miss Olson and Bobby Shaftoe but we learned to read. Mrs. Groves made up for lost time. She was stern, she found us wanting and lost her temper with us. Her face would grow red and more hair would escape from her hairnet when we failed miserably to live up to her demands. But we learned. And by the end of the school year we could read The Little Red Hen from front to back. And spell and sound out difficult words and add simple numbers and count to 100 and write all those numbers and many of those words. We were smart but tired and absolutely ready for summer vacation.

Miss Allen, Stella, was also one of my teachers, and there was no nonsense about just playing, or indulging in theatricals instead of the hard work of mastering reading, writing and arithmetic. But I don't want anyone to think school was dull or these were bad teachers. It wasn't; they weren't. We had lots of special events to look forward to every week. For one thing, on Fridays, those of us in the Little Room got to file across the hall, quietly of course, to the Big Room. And here we joined our older brothers and sisters and their friends in singing songs from *The Golden Book of Favorite Songs.* We sang about Old Dog Tray, Old Black Joe and Uncle Ned and we would get tears as we sang the words about laying down the shovel and the hoe and hanging up the fiddle and the bow. "For there's no more work for poor old Ned. He's gone where the good darkies go."

Remembering those words, I am shocked at their tone, their insensitivity to the black and white question. I suppose we didn't really know there was a question. The slaves were free, and we didn't have any "darkies" in our small world, so Uncle Ned might have been any of the old men who worked on farms around us, farmers themselves or their hired men,. except we didn't know too many who played the fiddle. But songs and stories were not always about the realities of daily life.

We sang too the songs of other lands, of *Kathleen Mavourneen, Flow Gently, Sweet Afton* and *Santa Lucia.* I loved them. And we sang about *The Old Oaken Bucket* and love songs such as "In the gloaming, oh my darling, when the lights are dim and low..." Ah, it was so sad, so beautifully sad. "Will you think of me and love me as you did once long ago? It was best to leave you thus. Best for you and best for me." What better preparation for the grown-up world of lost love and bittersweet partings?

And when we were all reduced to tears, we sang "Oh! the Bulldog on the Bank" who called the bullfrog a green old water fool and the monkey asked the owl, "Oh, what'll you have to drink?" And we ended that song laughing and tralalaing cheerfully and on to those resounding patriotic songs like *America* and *Battle Hymn of the Republic* and finally we were sent marching back to our own room to the tune of *Tramp, Tramp, Tramp* or *When Johnny Comes Marching Home*. *The Golden Book of Song*, what a treasure. Copyright 1915 and 1923. I still own one, I can still at least hum every song in it, two hundred or more.

We also had weekly meetings of our local chapter of the Young Citizens League where we learned about electing officers, appointing committees and taking on the jobs of keeping our schoolhouse and play yard clean and neat. And it was there we planned at least annual all-county Rally Days with sports competitions, and we also had joint meetings to plan county-wide educational projects, spelling bees and declamatory contests.

The young Citizens League was my father's idea while he was County Superintendent of Schools and it became a part of the state education plan. Wonderful for Dad, but it cost me my life in Mound City, for while I was in the fourth grade we moved to Pierre, the state capital, so that he could work in the Department of Education.

Keeping Up with Benny

ONE OF THE JOYS of first grade that I contemplated was a chance to play in the Rhythm Band. I had visited school and seen the children, my friends and neighbors, importantly accompanying the Victrola music with their rhythm sticks and sand blocks. They looked so competent and knowing up there in the front of the room, clicking their sticks and rubbing their blocks together in time to the music. Especially the Sousa marches—I loved those best—and the kids seemed able to relax and enjoy keeping time with them almost effortlessly.

We had no piano in the Little Room so the Victrola was our musical mainstay and our teacher worked hard to help us recognize the rhythms in the pieces she played. I had my turn with the sticks and the blocks and sometimes I got carried away and when I looked up, I thought I saw a rather pained expression on the teacher's face. I redoubled my efforts, twisted my face in concentration, my tongue was so often lodged between my teeth I forgot sometimes and bit down, drawing blood.

Then one day we heard the wonderful news—brand new instruments had arrived. The box was brought into the schoolroom and we were allowed to help unpack its precious contents. We gave new sticks and blocks only cursory attention, but then teacher drew forth the triangle, and next, two tambourines, and bird whistles and finally, a drum, a real drum. We gasped our delighted surprise. A drum! It was almost too much. And of course each of us secretly dreamed that we would be the one chosen to sit before that beauty with its real gut playing surface and the shiny chrome frame with the pale blue surround. It was beautiful.

Every day thereafter we gamely tried out on every instrument. We each took our turn on the familiar sticks and blocks, teacher's reminders ringing in our ears that these were the foundation of our orchestra and their importance must not be underestimated. We listened and we tried but we all wanted to be chosen to play the glamorous new additions, especially the drum. I tried, oh how mightily I tried, every ounce of me involved in blowing the bird whistle, shaking the tambourine, striking the triangle at just the right moment so that the note rang out on time, clear and sweet. And I banged that drum with vim and vigor.

Well, Benny Heisler got to be the drummer boy, Alice and Lydia blew the bird whistles, Pauline got the triangle and I was finally chosen to shake a tambourine. But it was a desperate choice made only because I couldn't be trusted on sticks nor blocks and I failed miserably at every other instrument. It was decided that it might be a good idea if I stood somewhat away from the rest of the band to shake "oh so gently, Elizabeth." The other tambourine player, I can't remember who it was, stood closer and was allowed to bang with more authority, usually safely drowning out my mistakes.

Still I never got tired of playing in that band and who knows, those efforts may have done something to improve my rhythm. I know one thing, my crush on Benny Heisler grew and grew every day as he mastered that drum and soon began playing with just the right beat at the right time. Such talent, such sophistication, I thought. And if I could only learn to shake the tambourine on time and with the proper reticence, I might be allowed to stand closer to him. I renewed my efforts.

October's Bright Days

HALLOWEEN TOOK ON SPECIAL SIGNIFICANCE at our house. It was my sister's birthday and although she might well have preferred decorations of pale blue and silver, what she got was pumpkins and black and orange. Her special celebration was inextricably mixed with the regular Halloween festivities. Usually there was a party in the school basement, with tubs of water for bobbing apples, skits and games which brought prizes to the creative. I still have my first costume, the orange and black dress my mother made for my sister and me, decorated with cutouts of black cats and jack o' lanterns.

We did not "trick or treat;" that was a custom I discovered much later. There was plenty of fudge and taffy and apples for treats, and the older kids took care of the tricks. Sometimes they managed to tie a few tin cans to someone's car, the sheriff's or the county superintendent of schools. We heard about window soaping but I never saw any evidence of it. Mostly, we all just milled around outside in the dark in an atmosphere of expectant excitement until our parents dragged us in to the school. Then we ate prodigiously, ran around noisily and finally collapsed, lumps to be stuffed into coats and hats and dragged home through the dark.

One November 1st morning, I woke to the sound of exclamations and muffled laughter downstairs. Dad was trying to decide how he felt about what he could plainly see from our front yard. The telephone had rung early and my parents were informed of what some declared an outrage and others thought was just plain funny, the high jinks of youth, no more.

I hurried downstairs to find out what was going on. Dad made me put on socks and my overshoes and then let me go outside to look. Clear against the first gray November morning sky—a wagon, like many a farmer rode in to town, sat on top of the schoolhouse roof.

How in the world did they do such a thing, some wondered. What possessed them, others muttered. What are we going to do about it, was the question Dad, the sheriff and other town fathers had to answer. Who did it was another question, but not a big one, there weren't very many possibilities. It wasn't long before practically everyone in town was dressed and outside, peering up at the wagon, half laughing, half indignant, but in all honesty, enjoying the excitement.

Now and then a voice rose in the crowd, and "outrage" or "ought to be in jail" could be heard. Mostly the rest of the crowd glanced impatiently at the speaker. Good heavens, no point in making a capital crime out of some Halloween nonsense. Just get the thing down and get on with it.

Get the thing down was one thing—how did it get up

there was another. The answer to that question was needed before the next step could be taken. It wasn't long before the culprits appeared accompanied by the sheriff and their embarrassed parents and we heard the magnitude of their daring. Half apologetic, half bragging, the red faced guilty boys told of taking the wagon apart, piece by piece, hauling it to the roof of the schoolhouse and reassembling it. All in the dead of night, the moon their only light, so silently they didn't wake a single person in the town.

Things were settled easily in those days, at least in Mound City. There were no arrests, no trials, nobody was labeled delinquent. The boys were admonished to "get the thing down, put it back together and return it to its owner." Hands were shaken, and a few heads, the town went back to breakfast, except the guilty, who went to work on the wagon on the roof.

Halloween was over once again, my sister's birthday a memory, the last of October's bright days had passed. But there was some secret smiling around town (you couldn't actually encourage that kind of thing, you know) and when people met on the street most of them chuckled together and cast an eye toward the schoolhouse to note the laborious process of removing the wagon.

Those darn kids, makes you feel kind of young again, by golly. Doesn't it?

Home Talent

IT IS NOT MY MEMORY that we were starved for entertainment in Mound City. We had church socials, Ladies Aid suppers, summer night games of Run Sheep Run for the children and we exchanged family dinners many a Sunday. If we were in our hired girl period or Grandma or Aunt Sis was staying with us, my parents had grown-up evenings of whist parties with refreshments. My mother loved cards and those were her favorite evenings. Dad, I think, preferred conversation and storytelling, at which he was a master.

We all looked forward to the home talent shows Dad and a few others put together at least once a year. There was music including the quartet in which he sang sometimes serious songs and romantic ones. *Danny Boy* was one I remember, for it always made me cry. Still does. They also sang nonsense songs, comic tunes like "K-K-K-Katie, when the m-m-moon shines over the c-c-c-cowshed, I'll be waiting at the k-k-k-kitchen door . . ." Sometimes there were minstrel acts, maybe whole minstrel shows, I'm not sure, but I can see men in black suits with black faces and hear them cracking jokes in a parody of how we thought "Negroes" talked.

I realize now how offensive those acts were, and the fact that they were done without malice is probably the most offensive thing about them. We certainly weren't sensitive, never mind politically correct. I suspect there were people in our county, probably among the hundred plus who lived in Mound City, who had never seen an African American. Certainly none lived there. Some years later when we lived in Pierre, there was one black resident—I think he shined shoes at the St. Charles Hotel. Whether he had a family, I confess with shame that I cannot remember if I ever knew. We were, I fear, an insular people, wrapped in our prairie cocoon.

The most detailed memory I have of a home talent show is the time Mac, the butcher, and Betty Alexander (they were later husband and wife, I think) sang, "Ruben, Ruben, I've been thinking what a fine world this would be, if the boys were all transported far beyond the Northern Sea." Ruben had his response of course, and they brought down the house. We giggled every time we saw them long after.

We left the courthouse basement on those evenings, spirits lifted, happier for a good laugh and the chance to be together. But even more important were the friendships forged and strengthened during the planning process, the rehearsals and preparations for the big night. Women were pressed to make costumes, and everyone in town soon came to recognize the furniture borrowed to decorate the stage for those occasions. It didn't take much to bring our front room to bare walls and my father often did that for home talent shows, plays he directed, and the traveling

Willis Kolodzie and Elizabeth (age 3) in the Tom Thumb wedding.

Home Talent: (back) Kathleen and Elizabeth, (front) Bob and Jack.

Bob, Jack and Buster the dog.

Denny Mills hauling water.

*Minnie Mills watering
her garden.*

*Elizabeth (age 5), Jack, Minnie
and Kathleen.*

"Those awful hats!" Kathleen, Jack and Elizabeth (age 5)

Elizabeth (age 7) and Aunt Lisette wearing bloomers cut down from men's trousers.

Aunt Sis with Bob.

The Parsonage

Standing on the only porch of the Parsonage: Kathleen, Jack and Elizabeth (age 6).

Bob, Jack, Elizabeth, Kathleen and the little red wagon.

Above: Harvest Scene c. 1900s

Left: Elizabeth (age 6) proudly poses with her new Bi-lo doll.

Elizabeth and Kathleen in their Easter finery.

Above: Before the Last Day (Kathleen, Bob, Jack and Elizabeth).

Below: Kathleen, Bob, Elizabeth and Jack in 1929 after the move to Pierre, SD.

Chautauqua which came to town every summer.

Chautauqua is a hazy memory. There was a big tent and the pews from the Methodist Church for seats. I got to wear my best dress every afternoon—poor Mother washed and ironed it every night. Suddenly the town was full of people. Farmers camped in town for the whole week if they had someone to leave at home to do the chores Relatives and friends came to visit family and other friends and take in the culture and of course there were the company members themselves to be invited home to dinner, to be followed and gazed at in awe and admiration.

There were lectures and I remember at least once someone dressed like William Jennings Bryan whose Cross of Gold speech rang out across the town. There was music—I seem to remember a cello solo. There were classes and discussion groups and plays. Again there went our furniture and that of other households and the audience sat enthralled in the dusty tent on the hard pew seats transported from our small town existence to something far more exotic.

One of the best features of Chautauqua, just as important as the imported culture, was the week of holiday spirit. Ordinary life was interrupted, women dressed up and tripped off every afternoon to take part in programs. Stores and businesses ran with rotating skeleton crews so men could do likewise. Farm families joined in the celebrations and there was a good deal of picnicking, visiting, and for all I knew, somewhere in the background perhaps an off-color story and a hidden whiskey bottle came into play. It was a good time, a happy time, a chance for usually housebound mothers to dress up and enjoy one another, for everyone to renew old friendships and make new ones, all in the name of improving oneself.

Kids loved it too. We felt grown-up and important all dressed up, sitting quietly, listening to a lot we didn't understand. And we could sneak off, after we changed into play clothes of course, and meet our friends behind the tent and escape the monitoring eyes of parents and neighbors who were too busy learning new things, "expanding their horizons," to worry about us. I suspect here first cigarettes were smoked, first swear words tried out loud, there was a lot of bragging and a few wrestling matches. We had the pure pleasure of dusty bare feet on warm dirt, sun on our shoulders, and the same feelings of conviviality that affected the grown-ups. Chautauqua was a great idea.

One summer became known among us as the summer of The Pageant. The Pageant was my father's dream and he enlisted the enthusiastic help of good people all around the county including many teachers to bring it into being. That spring every school practiced its part, grown-ups who were going to be settlers coming into the Territory and Indians from the Reservation rehearsed in their communities. Dad and his helpers traveled to the river and marked the spots where various parts of the pageant would take place. On the big day we all trekked to the river, donned our costumes: I was a pansy, my brother Jack was a bumble bee and my sister got to be a glamorous butterfly. The flowers waved and nodded in the grass, birds and butterflies hovered, the settlers' wagons rolled in, cows and buffalo stampeded and the Indians came whooping, riding their horses and dancing in a great circle, and the cameras rolled. Somehow my father had managed to get the Fox Film Company, a real Hollywood movie maker, to film our efforts. The pageant dramatized the history of our county, Campbell County, glossing over our treatment of the Indians, but we were all impressed.

After the pageant we gratefully shed our costumes and feasted royally on fried chicken and other treats the county's mothers had packed, audience and actors indistinguishable from one another celebrated together. My father was happy and his family was proud of his success.

I would like to think a can of film still exists, hidden away somewhere, that the Fox Film Company took of our mighty endeavors and which we all saw in the movie theater in Mobridge, our neighboring city of three, perhaps even four thousand people. The accompanying film was something with Mary Pickford—silent of course, interesting—but we were all more taken with our own roles and our friends' and neighbors' in The Pageant.

November

⁓

NOVEMBER WAS A DOUR MONTH on the prairie with lower ing skies and frozen ground mostly unsoftened by snow. In my memory, it was the month in which we saw the least sunshine, when climbing out of the covers in the early morning dark held little promise. I would lie there curled about myself, lingering in the warmth and body smells of the bed I shared with my sister or Martha, our hired girl, to sift through the possibilities of a dark day.

The early morning house would still be cold when I finally had to get up. We would eat our oatmeal by kerosene lamplight and wrapped in heavy coats and scratchy wool scarves, overshoes clinking, my sister and I would grab our syrup pails in mittened hands and head off across town to get the morning milk. Cold was different without brilliant sunshine, with no snow masking the frozen mud. It pierced and made you shiver and instead of sending you in wild abandoned running to get warm, it made you huddle and shake inside your clothes. There were no bird tracks, no prints of tiny animal feet to follow. Even Buster watched for a moment as we headed down the road and then returned to his place by the kitchen stove. Our bearing must have told him this would not be a rollicking journey, no fun, just work.

The schoolroom was dark these mornings, the teacher's voice sharp, insistent, urging us out of our apathy. Our winter woolens scratched, our noses dripped, and our eyes were vacant. Finally in desperation, she called for morning exercise and we stood beside our desks ready to jump, feet apart, hands overhead, one and two and faster now, faster, she would press us to get the blood moving and wake us from our dullness.

After school, the coal tubs filled and hauled to the house on our brother's red wagon and any other outdoor chores finished, we huddled around the kitchen table watching Mother skim the soup and take the gingerbread from the oven. If she was baking bread, her white arms would flash in the light of the kerosene lamp that lit our dark kitchen.

Comfort foods were our rewards for enduring winter's first dark cold days. Breakfast cocoa hiding under its milk skin, and before bed the wire popcorn popper crackling with its snowy treasure, then coated with golden butter, helped us forget the chilly dimness of the days and remember the bright ones which would come when we could skim across the snowy fields on sleds that were freshly varnished, waiting, ready.

On the 11th day of November, Armistice Day, we called it, at eleven o'clock in the morning, lessons halted and we rose and placed our hands over our hearts while the bugler in his old army uniform played the military retreat and taps. For the rest of the day we sang the songs our fathers and uncles and their home folks had sung during the Great War. *Over There*, we sang, and *Pack Up Your Troubles in the Old Kit Bag and Smile, Smile, Smile.* And of course *America, the Beautiful* and *My Country Tis of Thee* and *Star Spangled Banner.* We took turns reciting the poetry of war and reconciliation, it didn't matter which war, and in every way that a room full of six to ten years olds could, we praised and honored those who had gone to the war to end war. At last, the teacher wound the Victrola and, waving the paper flags we had colored and pasted to sticks of wood, we marched around the schoolroom in our final gesture of respect and admiration and then, grabbing our coats and caps, out the door and home.

Now the last of the Canada geese flew their arrow formations above us honking across the gray skies. The prairie winds turned colder, sometimes blowing up a flurry of frozen moisture, more sleet than snow. Our cheeks grew red and chapped, our lips stung. Our house took on its winter smell of wool and cooking cabbage and bodies closely wrapped against the cold. Evenings after schoolwork was done, instead of our usual card and board games, we began the preparations for the holiday ahead.

The bag of pine cones imported from the Black Hills, far away, and saved from year to year, came out of its hiding place and with carefully colored paper heads, bits of red cloth for the wattles and crows' feathers we had gathered for tails, we made Thanksgiving turkeys to decorate the table for the feast to come. We debated solemnly the advantages of turkey over goose or chicken for that special dinner. And we discussed the recipe for dressing, no oysters, please, Mother, and whether sweet potatoes should have marshmallows (no!) and gravy, please, lots and lots of good brown gravy, and potatoes mashed with real cream, and cranberry sauce, and a plate of dill pickles and carrots from the fruit cellar restored to crispness with icy water from the well. With luck there would be the rare winter treat of celery and, of course, our favorite green beans dressed with bacon and vinegar.

And pie! No one could outdo our mother's pies, the crusts so crisp, so short, so mouth melting, two with spicy sour cream raisin filling, two with pumpkin. Plenty for seconds and before bed snacks.

But first, of course, came the schoolroom celebrations, our pilgrim costumes, the boys with their high crowned, black paper hats which I envied, although I liked the lace trimmed cap my mother made for me out of an old pillow slip, and we all had cardboard buckles painted silver which almost covered our shoes. The luckiest kids, I thought, were the boys who got to be Indians, their faces painted, a single feather, the longest one a rooster could spare, tucked under a leather bootlace headband, and a bright blanket slung across their shoulders. Funny, I don't remember any Indian girls, their dress was not colorful enough, I suppose, their role in the festivities considered too dull.

The holiday feast behind us, November dragged to a close. Now each morning we rose to peek out our frosty windows hoping for the sight of a clean white snow quilt to cover the dun colored earth. We were eager for sleds and snowballs and we counted the days until Christmas.

Messengers

WE WERE ON OUR WAY to my grandmother's house. Our car was parked beside the road and the family milled around waiting for my mother to change the baby's diaper. I saw Jack toddling near the car suddenly disappear and then come struggling out of the ditch on all fours. My sister peered down at him and held out her hand. My father poured a cup of coffee from the thermos, stretched and took his hat off to rub his head. I ran through the stubble field, my jacket bellying in the wind like a kite on the verge of flying until I found myself on a gentle crowning hill.

The world smelled of the coming snow and the sharp bite of Russian thistles someone was burning. It was so quiet where I stood that I could hear my own breath and when I closed my eyes I felt dizzy. It was a strange sensation to stand in the middle of the prairie, unbroken horizon on every side. I thought that I could feel the earth turning, spinning on its axis and I was alone in the emptiness. I closed my eyes and held my jacket out on either side swaying with the rhythm of the universe, the wind softly singing its song of earth and sky.

Then came the distant sound of honking and I looked up to see arrows of Canada geese overhead. I could hear their wings fanning the air. Probably they would settle soon on a nearby marsh to feed on the remnants of the wheat harvest. I had seen them there once, and heard them, noisily calling to one another, scolding over territory, so many of them the marsh looked alive, undulating in the early evening.

My father had explained their presence to me, but I wanted to ignore his information about where they landed and how they fed and where they were going and why. I only wanted to think of them flying, free, going forever through the wind and the clouds, looking down in pity on the earth-bound. Snowflakes touched my nose and my lips, I licked them and closed my eyes again to feel the earth spin beneath me and the wind lift my hair. Then I opened my eyes to see the geese heading away from me toward the south. Real or imagined, there would be for a long time the faint sound of their honking in my ears, an invitation, I thought, to join them. In church, they kept saying to listen to God's word, to "heed the call." I had never heard it before, perhaps this was it. I rose to my tiptoes and stretched and flapped my jacket wings, waiting to leave the earth, to rise and fly with them.

"Liz-a-beth," my mother's voice summoned me, and I turned toward the car and my family. They seemed far away, disconnected, but the geese were disappearing too, only faintly visible, then finally gone. Wherever they were going I was with them, a lord of the air, riding the clouds somewhere between Mound City and God.

First Snow

~

WE COULD NEVER BE SURE how winter would come to the prairie. Sometimes it grew out of a long series of sullen, gray, late autumn days and frosty nights, each colder, bleaker than the last. The ground froze in icy swales and hummocks and the stubbly grass became silver needles which snapped beneath our feet.

Sometimes a sudden icy blast from the north brought the same results in a matter of minutes. The dry prairie wind sucked the moisture from every living thing, leaving our skin rough, cracked and exquisitely sensitive. Last year's chilblains began to sting heralding a long painful season. Lips cracked and bled and no one left the house without the lengthy rites of bundling and mittening. Scarves muffled our mouths and noses leaving only slits for eyes.

I stopped complaining about the long underwear and the below knee black bloomers. Laboriously, I wrapped and folded the underwear legs at my ankles, anchoring them into position with one hand while I pulled long black cotton stockings up over them, and bloomer legs down to cover garters which were supposed to keep stockings from droop-ing. But I drooped, I sagged and I bunched, my skinny legs taking on the appearance of heavily bandaged varicosities.

The last honking Canada geese had long since veed across our skies. My father had piled the mixture of dirt and manure around the base of our house to keep icy winds from invading. The coal pile in the shed was heaped high, the galvanized tubs conveniently near. The red wagon was parked and waiting.

One morning, we would wake to a silence that even the youngest of us could recognize, and we rushed bare-foot across the icy wood floors to peer through frost pat-terned windows at a world transformed. A shimmering white quilt, hemstitched with the tracks of winter birds, covered everything. At best plain most of the year, with the first snow our town was transformed into a picture book village. The angularity of the harsh landscape was rounded, soft to the eye, hushed to the ear. Common objects took on magic. The pump had a new, white-spined handle; cornstalks which had bent to the wind, now lay plump, white on white. Dia-monds glinted on roof ridges; frozen loco weed and Rus-sian thistles sparkled in the sun.

Morning cocoa burned our tongues and still chewing slabs of oven toast frosted with melting butter, we began the task of winding and wrapping ourselves into layers of outer wear. Mother enforced galoshes and double mittens.

At last, we rushed out the back door and then stood for a few moments, fleeing animals caught in the glare of a bright light. We were captured and frozen still by the beauty before our eyes. The sun had risen far above the horizon and every weed, every stem and stick was encrusted with fairy gems. Nothing moved. It was as if the world had stopped breathing. Evidence of man's presence was gone, covered, masked by the clean, sun-struck whiteness of snow.

Something always broke the spell, a dog loping across the vacant lot next door, a car or horse and wagon on the road. And then we went screaming, careening into the shimmering white world to break the silence, to prove that we were there, that we lived. We made snowballs and scraped the snow from fence rails and kicked it from Russian thistles. We rolled in the precious, pure, cold whiteness and thrashed our arms to create angel wings.

We tramped out our circles for a quick game of Fox and Geese, and slid off our mittens to feel the dry, white cold and then the trickle of melting snow on our wrists and up our sleeves. We tasted. The snow was dry, powdery, it almost tasted like dust. The cleanest dust in the world.

There was something manic, hysterical, about our response to this first snow of the season. Experience told us it would soon be stained with coal dust and dirt that blew in from fields plowed and left fallow months earlier. Its beauty would be tainted with the footprints of the town going about its business.

Our mother would call and send us off with syrup pails to get the morning milk. Our father would remind us to bring in the coal. And the school bell would ring us back to our accustomed daily labors. The gems of winter would melt into mud.

But soon, if not this time, the snow would come to stay and we could haul out our battered sleds and fly whooping down the pasture slope onto Heisler's frozen pond. And then lie abed to dream of days to come, when grass would be green and bluebells would bloom again on the prairie.

Christmas Bells

⌒

IT WAS DARK, almost too dark to make out the shapes of my
brothers in their cots. Beside me, my sister lay still, breathing quietly. Moonlight glowed dimly through the thick frost
on our attic bedroom window. I listened for sound, hoping
to hear my father rattling the coal stove downstairs, claw-
ing out the clinkers and shaking the ashes ready for a new
fire. All was quiet, there was no smell of coffee. My mother
wasn't in the kitchen stirring up pancakes.

I lay still under my mound of covers, army blankets,
Grandma's quilt, and the much washed braided wool rug
necessary to keep us warm on winter nights. Someday, I
promised myself, someday I will have a feather bed, two
feather beds, one to sleep on and one to cover myself with.

The silence was thick around me. Suddenly I knew, it
was the silence of snow, snow that muffled all sound. There
were no wagon wheels, no cars, no squeaking footsteps.
Not even a dog barked; no far-away coyote sang. I debated
with myself about getting up, braving the icy floor to scratch

171

a clear spot on the window pane so I could see. I loved the sight of new snow's clean whiteness, unmarked by wheels or footprints. I would wrap myself warm and watch the sky lighten, see the first bird tracks, the yellow stain that Anderson's dog would leave by the skinny plum tree. For just a little while, minutes perhaps, It would be my world out there, without anyone, not even the lights of other houses to take it from me.

That moment the church bells rang, breaking the snowy silence, pealing out across the landscape. And I remembered. It was Christmas, Christmas morning, and our Lord was born, the minister had said so.

"When you hear the bells ring at midnight, you will know that Christ is born. He has come to save us."

It was midnight. No wonder my father wasn't building the fire and my mother stirring pancake batter. The night was only half over, it would be hours and hours before I could steal downstairs and look at my stocking. I forgot the mystery of Christ's birth. I forgot the dream of claiming the silent world for my own. I wanted morning, I wanted my sister and brothers to wake, I wanted Christmas, I wanted presents, one present.

Would it be there, the Bi-lo baby doll I longed for? I pictured its fine bisque head with painted golden hair and sky-blue eyes that opened and closed. I could see the long white batiste dress and slip trimmed with lace and the tiny bonnet, just as I had seen them in the catalogue a hundred, a thousand times. I had peeked at it every morning before school and hugged it to me when I came home even before I changed my school clothes. It lay open on the old round kitchen table while I practiced writing my letters and numbers, and it resided now under my pillow where I had put it every night since the catalogue came.

"She's too young, Denny," I had heard my mother say, "she'll break it the first week. You know how she is." They thought I was outdoors with the other kids.

I was clumsy, I knew that. I moved too fast, my father said. I got too excited, and forgot to think. I broke things, dropped them and stepped on them and carried them outdoors to keep them near me and then forgot and they suffered from sun or rain and snow. I loved things to death—I heard my mother tell my grandmother that.

But I wanted that baby doll. What a loving mother I would be. I would never let anything I loved so much suffer from thoughtlessness or neglect. I was confused about Santa Claus, did he make the decision, or did my parents? I knew they would have a great deal of influence on him. He wouldn't bring presents they didn't approve.

I lay in the silent dark, wishing my sister would wake. There was no doubt she would get what she wanted, paints and books and hair ribbons. And if she had been the one wanting my doll, it would have been no problem, for she was neat and careful. She loved having her pretty yellow hair brushed, her dresses almost never had spots, her black cotton stockings were always pulled up smoothly over her long underwear. Mine bunched into ugly knots, my dark brown hair snarled and I hated the hair brush.

Prayers of hope and promises of perfection kept me company in the dark cold. Oh God, if I can please have that doll, I'll never ask for another thing. Never. And I'll polish my shoes and take my nasty cod-liver oil and wash my hands before I eat. I will. I promise. And I won't hate my sister because her eyes are like bluebells.

I fell asleep, dreaming of a perfect child, cheerful, sweet-tempered, who dried dishes without complaint nor breakage, and endlessly entertained her younger brothers so her mother could rest. Her spelling pages were perfect, none of her picture books were dog-eared or torn, and inexplicably, she had long blond hair and cornflower-blue eyes.

Minutes later it seemed, I heard my father's voice booming from the kitchen downstairs.

"Merry Christmas, everyone up. Santa Claus has been here."

She was there under the tree, my beautiful Melanie Marie, the name I had chosen months ago. She lay in a cradle made of a basket I recognized; it always sat on top of the glass cupboard to be brought out for special occasions, to hold Christmas cards or Easter eggs. Now it had a soft, shiny pink lining and a tiny pillow.

My brothers loaded their toy trucks with pine needles from the Christmas tree, my sister danced in her new blue dress, and I, I sat transfixed with my new baby. My mother gave me a white towel to use as a baby blanket. "It's too big, honey," she said. "I'll make you a better one soon."

I wrapped her and unwrapped her a hundred times, and all through breakfast my doll lay cocooned in her blanket next to my place where I could pat her and reassure myself that she was real. When my Aunt Lisette and Grandma came hoo-hooing at the back door bringing armloads of ribboned packages, I jumped to my feet and grabbed for Melanie Marie. Somehow, I failed to hold on to the rolled up towel and she slipped to the floor, her tiny head shattered into pieces. The china-blue eyes gazed up at me.

That very same doll lies in a box on my closet shelf with the new head my parents found for her. Her hair and eyes are brown. I learned to love her.

New Year's Eve

CHRISTMAS WAS OVER, the aura of expectancy disappeared with it. Life was just as good as ever, but it lacked star shine and candle glow, presents and ah yes, lots of chocolate. Everyone in the family was tired, probably we all had colds. The miracle of fresh snow was often replaced with blotchy heaps of gray, dirtied by blowing dust and chimney soot. Daytime temperatures lifted enough so that snow melted leaving muddy little ponds everywhere, nights it froze solid and icicles hung from every eave ready to drip down your neck when you ventured outside.

By now there were more needles on the rug than on the Christmas tree and even surrounded by adults and pails of water and sand, we were no longer allowed to light the candles for even a minute. The sugar cookie cache was getting very low, the big box of Fannie Farmer's chocolates had disappeared. Siblings were getting on each other's nerves, and Mother needed a break.

One thing worked, a reminder that the New Year's Day

feast was coming and the celebration of New Year's Eve was imminent. I hoped we would have brown crusty roast pork nestled in a bed of equally brown sauerkraut with mashed potatoes and gravy and Grandma's sour cream raisin pie. And I clamored to be allowed to stay up on New Year's Eve until the magic hour of twelve. No amount of argument or distraction by my mother swayed me. Yes, I would stay awake. Yes, I would walk to my own bed up the stairs and into the cold and not expect my father to carry me. I would fill my own hot water bottle and put it in my bed before-times and would not complain of the cold. I would, I would, I would.

As the special evening progressed we ate hot buttered popcorn from the old wire popper shaken over the coal range or sometimes the front room base burner. We drank cocoa and devoured the last of the Christmas cookies, ate the Christmas orange from our stockings that we had been saving, and sucked the ribbon candy bestuck with bits of thread and who knows what from the toe of that same stocking where it had been hidden all week.

Wrapped in blankets and pillows borrowed from our beds, we curled up on the floor by the stove to wait for the magic moment when Dad would slip out ring the church bells. First came twelve portentous tolls to mark the hour and remark the year passed and welcome the new one. Then there was a frenzied klaxon of ringing to wish joy and happiness and we were allowed to stick our noses outside and bang a kettle lid and shout good wishes. But the cold sent us back to our blankets and even as the noise mounted, we began to nod.

Next thing I knew, I was being guided to a cold bed, for I had forgotten my hot water bottle. No matter, I had stayed awake for the bells and tomorrow's feast lay ahead. My New Year's resolutions were . . . but it was too late, I was asleep.

Someone's Valentine

IT IS ONE OF LIFE'S GREAT MYSTERIES why someone way back when chose January as the beginning of the New Year. January never seemed so much a beginning as an end. The prairie lay frozen and inert under a blanket of dirty snow. Viruses (although I don't think we knew to call them by that name) that had been lurking off-stage, made their entrance and we coughed and sniffled, always searching for the rag, a torn piece of sheet perhaps, that passed for a handkerchief.

The first snow, Christmas, and New Years were over; holiday candles had burned out. January was a tired month and February could be just as gray and cold. The chores of winter seemed endless. We hauled the coal and braved icy winds to fetch the milk. Lamp chimneys must be washed right after school for lamps were lit early to combat the winter dark.

This is the month when the only childhood memories I can muster are of ice and sleep and long underwear. And valentines. Valentines saved February. Valentine's Day was more than a day; it took its place among the seasons by which we marked our lives. Days ahead we began the search for materials to make the works of art we would give to our teacher and our friends. We knew we would be called upon to remember our parents with our handiwork at school.

Every bit of lace, the crocheted edging from an old pillow case, sheets of red construction paper and oddments of other colors, bits of silk and embroidery floss, dried flowers, even fur, and pictures from last years seed catalogues and the best of Sears Roebuck and "Monkey Wards" were hoarded. Envied was the one who had access to a wallpaper sample book or left over doilies from some ladies luncheon, and how we fought over Mother's old copies of Delineator Magazine.

Finally it was time, and one evening after supper dishes were done, we were allowed to mix the flour and water paste to which we added a few drops of peppermint flavoring to make it less obnoxious. My parents knew it would end up on the chairs, the floor, the table and on me. I cut and colored and pasted messily, chewed my tongue in concentration and smoothed my hair with pasty fingers. The fanciest valentines with flowers and frills were for my best beloveds, some kids I fear, got short shrift with a just a red heart, a bit of white doily in the center and another smaller heart smacked on in haste. It was the unwritten but strictly enforced rule at our house that everyone in the schoolroom was to get a valentine. Some I simply signed with my name, no sentimental messages. They went to classmates I liked well enough but in whom I had no romantic interest or who were not, at the moment at least, best friends.

For the ones I loved, Willis and Benny and Sonny, my

dearest friend Pauline, and our teacher, Miss Dynan, there were much fancier versions with snatches of poetry painstakingly copied from a book and entreaties to "Be Mine, Valentine," as well as promises to be theirs.

The morning of the big day we arrived to find the walls and blackboard covered with red chalk hearts and legends of love. We struggled to pay attention to the capitals of Italy and France, the rivers of South America or the new words in The Little Red Hen. That afternoon lessons were put aside, desks cleared and the party began. Mothers shed their coats and hats and smiled sweetly as they served heart shaped cookies with pink frosting and punch made of home canned fruit juices decorated with precious slices of orange.

All morning we had stared at the "valentine box," ruffled and wrapped in red crepe paper with white doves and ribbon bows, into which we had all dropped our precious hand-made beauties. We were beside ourselves with suspense. How many, we each wondered, are there for me. Will I be forgotten? As a reward for especially good behavior, one lucky, self-important kid was allowed to come forward and read the names. We were all in an emotional turmoil although we tried to keep our faces bland, our bodies still. If we didn't get many or any valentines, we certainly didn't want anyone to know we cared. Kid stuff, boring, our shrugs must indicate.

Now I recognized my parents' wisdom in making sure I had a valentine for everyone. Why hadn't I made one for myself? Would Sonny and Willis and Benny remember me, or would they pass me by for Alice or Pauline. The cookies were flour dust in my mouth, the punch without flavor.

We blushed and struggled to the front of the room when our names were called while the rest foot-shuffled, whispered, and whistled cat calls. Finally the last beautiful card was distributed; the teacher had seen to it that everyone got valentines and it was apparent there were other good moms in Mound City. Surreptitiously we counted, looked for the important names and figured out the "guess who's." I was happy. The ones I loved, loved me. At least today—this time. Who cared if they loved Alice and Pauline and Lydia too? I loved them all.

The second round of cookies was delicious, the punch was nectar. Vigorously we sang the songs teacher chose for the occasion, *Red, Red Robin* and *Believe Me If All Those Endearing Young Charms*. We stood at attention and chanted in unison to the helping mothers, "Thank you Mrs. Kluckman, thank you Mrs. Kundert and Mrs. Mills." We thanked our teachers and grabbed a last cookie.

And then we were free, rushing pell-mell into the muddy schoolyard, shrieking our excitement, madly pushing and shoving one another. We had to touch, we needed one more reassurance that we were alive and we were loved.

Giddy in the winter sunshine, we raced along the rutted tracks, our coats and scarves open to the wind, to share our treasures at home. We were someone's valentine, they were ours. To be loved was wondrous, to love even more wonderful.

Losing Tonsils

~

MOTHER WAS TIRED and discouraged at the end of a long winter of croup. whooping cough, measles, and miscellaneous illnesses that had kept me out of school and ailing for weeks. It was decided that I should have my tonsils out. Our good Dr. Volleben hoped that might make me stronger and more disease resistant.

The hospital was a big old house in Mobridge, about thirty miles from Mound City. We duly reported there one morning. I remember standing in what had once been the front room, all dark wood and lace curtains, wondering what would happen next, scared but curious too. A doctor, a stranger, pot-bellied and important, examined me carefully, tweaked my nose and instructed the starchy nurse to get me ready. I remember feeling not just small but like one of the Teeny Weenies in my favorite book next to that plump, white-clad, red-faced nurse. Her cap was so stiff and shiny the light bounced off of it like another sun. She was kind but firm and I was unceremoniously stripped of my clothes, bundled into a funny nightgown and led to a room with a high, hard white table-bed and big lights. I'm sure I was frightened, but I was also very interested and didn't cry. That was a rule in our house—visits to doctors and dentists were necessary, you could complain before and after, but during you kept a stiff upper lip and dry eyes.

While he was waiting for me, the doctor gave my sister a going over and it was decided that she might as well have the surgery too—a kind of two-for-one arrangement. Not only was she horrified and angry at this turn of events, she blamed me, and it was a long time before I was forgiven for leading her to this moment. Part of me sympathized with her. It didn't seem fair to have this decision come when she was so unprepared, but part of me rejoiced—we would share the discomfort.

The surgeries went well. I enjoyed the ice cream I was given as soon as I woke. I slept soundly that night and the next morning had only a sore throat, but I had had those before and I was ready to leave when our parents came to get us. Kathleen had not fared so well. She was nauseated all night, couldn't keep the ice cream down and she hurt, not moderately as I did, but really hurt. Understandably, she was not happy.

The doctor said her discomfort would pass, there was no bleeding, we were both in quite good shape to travel, and we were loaded in the car. Off we went to grandma's house—a fifty mile drive. I guess I slept most of the time in the car and felt well enough when we got to Grandma's to eat a fried chicken dinner with mashed potatoes and sour cream pie. Kathleen lolled disconsolately on the horsehair sofa sipping an egg nog, watching me with angry eyes.

It was one of life's little ironies that I, the puny child, recovered both health and spirits without delay and

Kathleen, always a bit more robust, had a much more difficult time. It was our first and last encounter with a hospital for a very long time. Something— Dr. Volleben's tonic in cherry wine, the tonsillectomy or just the passage of time— brought on some improvement in my health and Mother and Dad were sure they had done the right thing in my case. I think they may have doubted their wisdom when it came to Kathleen. She took a long time to recover from the onslaught—not just on her body, but on something else—her psyche perhaps. She hadn't been prepared to have surgery, no one had convinced her of its necessity and she resented us all for her suffering.

Gilding the Lily

⌒

THERE WERE TWO CHURCHES in Mound City—the Methodist, to which we were neighbor, and the Lutheran,
across town. I'm sure their congregations celebrated Easter in traditional religious fashion, but I remember very
little about that. What I do remember is that Easter was the
wardrobe turning point—it marked the onset of spring.
And no matter what the weather, the expected intermit-
tent showers and sun, cold, dismal rain or an unseasonable
norther bearing down with snow and ice, we decked ourselves out in spring finery for the day.

The long underwear that itched and twisted around
us all winter came off. True, it might go back on Monday if
the weather didn't clear, but for Easter Sunday, it came off.
With it went the voluminous black bloomers and the woolly
petticoats. Out came our light tan or pale blue spring coats
with their hems turned down; poor Mother labored for
hours with wet pressing cloth and the sadiron heated on
the coal stove to obliterate history. Shorten it for this one,

lengthen it for the other.

The only thing that wasn't different was our shoes—the shiny black patent leather Mary Janes which were liberally coated with Vaseline every minute they weren't on our feet, sufficed as Sunday wear the year around. Two pair of dress shoes exceeded our resources and besides, "they weren't necessary." That is a phrase heard often where we lived. Even those who could afford it didn't splurge unnecessarily.

Our long black stockings gave way to light colored knee socks or anklets with a touch of lace, our underpants were light cotton and our slips cotton knit. Over this went our new dresses—my sister's and mine. Mother was not always so fortunate—by the time she had her four children suitably attired, there was neither time nor energy for anything for herself. My sister and I always had new dresses if you didn't count that they came from a garment formerly owned by someone else, a generous aunt, perhaps. But my mother was a master of insets and gussets and ruffles cut on the bias from scraps, or pleats which covered unwanted seams, a choice bit of embroidery to distract the eye. Unless you knew the history, we had new clothes for Easter, and so did my brothers. Theirs were made over from some male relative's cast offs or from a yardage remnant that came to us somehow.

I remember a favorite dress of mine. It was creamy white with a scattering of tiny colored print flowers. Mother watched me with an eagle eye every minute that I wore it, for washing it was a demanding business. And ironing it at least as difficult. That meant I was only allowed to wear it for a strictly limited time—to church probably, and then had to change into everyday play clothes—but still lightweight spring kinds of things.

I remember how sweetly that dress slipped against my body, how light and silky it felt as I moved. My father was always after me to stand straight, "Shoulders back, Elizabeth," for I had the natural tendency of skinny kids to hunch, especially under the burden of heavy winter clothes. But when I wore that dress I stood so proudly, moved so gracefully to feel it swish against my legs, he found no need to caution me. My bare arms were winter white and probably covered with goosebumps if the temperature disappointed, as it almost always did, but I felt light as air and pretty as a rose in that dress.

The last, the final touch to my Easter wardrobe was a hat, the traditional Easter bonnet. Mother made these too, or at least retrimmed old ones so that we felt they were new. One I remember was somebody's straw hat, a cloche it was called, maybe my last year's one, which she covered with pale silk vertical bands, like georgette, and tied with a ribbon band. It sat low on my head and probably I didn't see very well from under it, but I was sure I was not only as well turned out as any little girl in the pattern books my mother followed, but more beautiful than most.

I can see us now, my handsome parents and their four children dressed in Easter finery. There was a final inspection, a straightening of collars, last words of advice about behavior. The lisle stocking tops made into stretchy little caps that were holding their pompadours in place were whisked from my little brothers' still damp heads and we headed out the door into spring, to celebrate.

Chances are we had the traditional ham dinner as part of our Easter celebration and in all probability we shared that meal with friends. We often did, my father loved company and my mother gamely produced tasty meals on our old coal range despite the care of four small children. Part of me hated to take off my beautiful finery to protect it from spills and dribbles, although another part of me reveled in the freedom from worry of play clothes. But to gild the skinny lily just a little, I might insist on a hair ribbon. These were huge ribbon bows like giant butterflies which were anchored to the tops of our heads by a hank of hair threaded through a gold ring and secured with a sturdy rubber band. I yelled loudly at the twisting, complaining of intolerable pain, but quieted when Mother said fine, maybe we'd just forget the ribbon. No, I needed a bit of decoration to mark the specialness of the day.

No matter the Easter weather, no matter if we were buttoned into our long underwear once more on Monday if the cold winds blew, spring was coming and not a moment too soon.

Turning Dead

◦—

IT SEEMED TO ME there was a lot of dying going on during our Mound City years. Both of my grandfathers died and although I didn't get to see my Grandpa Mills very often since he lived far away in Minneapolis, I missed knowing he was there. He was the source of so many good stories Dad and his brothers and sisters told, I didn't want them to stop. My Aunt May told me about when Grandpa was living with her and he came home one night very late and what she called, in his cups. Aunt May climbed out of bed to answer his loud knock and looked out the window just in time to see Mr. O'Reilly who ran the local mortuary drive off. Grandpa kept banging on the door and when Aunt May finally got downstairs to open it she must have given him a pretty cold shoulder for Grandpa tipped his hat, eased by her unsteadily and said, "Pardon me for livin', I just fell out of a hearse," and stumbled off to bed. It's a much funnier story when told in the Irish brogue that all of the Mills clan could put on when the occasion demanded.

189 / Turning Dead

Another time, he came home saying he had met Mr. Connoly downtown and gone with him to his house for "a drop." Mr. Connoly had been building his house for years, adding room upon room in strange and awkward patterns so that halls came to an end with no doors as if they had forgotten where they were going and roofs looked as if they would run into one another but never quite met. "Oh indeed," Grandpa said, (although he actually said something like "indaid") "he's got a fine puzzlin' garden there."

Grandpa Kusler had been sick for a long time but his death still came as a surprise to me. All death did. I simply couldn't see how such a thing could happen to people close to me—in China maybe or strange places like Albuquerque, New Mexico, but not in Mound City or anywhere else to my people.

I remember the day Uncle Ruh died, he was my mother's great uncle, a minister. He was a rather dim figure to me, always in a black suit and a round kind of black hat and very white shirt. Tante, his wife, Mother's great aunt, was a tiny woman always garbed in black too and it seemed to me always with a basket on her arm. Tante spent her life visiting the poor and the sick in the little town where they lived. The news of Uncle's death is forever associated with the day Mother decided to cut my hair. She was tired of dealing with the eternal snarls in my long hair that she tried to keep curled with rags and of my bleating complaints when she tried to get a comb through them. So that day out came the scissors and in minutes I ended up with what we called a Buster Brown haircut after the little figure that appeared on the inside of Buster Brown shoes.

Just as Mother finished snipping, the old wall telephone rang and the operator, Mrs. Falde no doubt, announced that it was long distance from Leola. Long distance, even fifty miles of distance, almost inevitably meant bad news. Only occasionally one of our richer relatives called from the city even if no one had died. Most times, good news could wait for a letter and letters came almost daily from someone, Grandma, Uncle Ernest, friends a few miles away.

It was Mother's Uncle Ernest calling to tell us that Uncle Ruh was dead. Mother told me to run up to school and tell Dad the sad news and I tore out into the sunshine, heady with the freedom of my new haircut. Probably I wasn't very sad but I was very excited about my new look and I failed to see the wire stretched across the rutty drive into the schoolyard and ran smack into it, bruising my throat and sending me into a heap on the ground. Once Dad was sure my wounds weren't serious and he got over the shock of Uncle's demise, he cast disappointed eyes on my hair. The only words he could get out were something like, "What have you done?" Dad liked long hair and his upset at my bowl cut was small stuff beside the way he reacted when my mother followed fashion and bobbed her long dark locks. She stuck a barrette in the side of the shorn tresses and even I thought the look did lack something.

These were the days when there were no antibiotics and vaccinations were just beginning to be in widespread use. My sister and brothers and I were the first children in our county to get some of these vaccinations. It was too late to save me from whooping cough but we escaped diphtheria and small pox. Measles and scarlet fever were common and occasionally a child died of the complications of one of those, or suffered permanent side effects such as diminished eyesight and hearing. Because of the danger, homes with a sick child diagnosed with any serious communicable disease were quarantined—red signs on a house warned others not to come in and the residents not to go out. Fathers often had to move into other quarters so they could continue to work and mothers were left alone to contend with one sick child after another until the disease had run its course.

Babies died at birth and all too often mothers died with them or soon after. Babies who successfully survived that hurdle were prone to illnesses often called summer complaint. Violent diarrhea and vomiting, if it couldn't be checked in time, stole those tiny lives.

My friend Buddy Kolodzie was terribly burned and after weeks in the hospital he sat wrapped in a sheet in front of his parents' pool hall/ice cream parlor/candy store. We were all proud of Buddy for cheating death and made it a point to go by and see him where he held court on the wooden sidewalk watching people and cars go by, getting greetings from young and old alike.

It was the custom to have flower girls at funerals in Mound City. I have never heard of that tradition anywhere else but my sister and I always had to have a white dress, winter and summer, suitable for our role as flower carriers at the final rites for Mound City residents who passed on. We were lined up outside or in the vestibule of the church with our sheaves of flowers and ferns until the mourners were all seated and then we paraded down the aisle to place our bouquets carefully on the coffin if there was room or on the floor beside it. We took our seats in the front row, four or six or more of us, depending upon the importance of the deceased I expect, and waited until the rites came to an end. I listened to the hymns and sometimes the words about the dead person, but often I simply dreamed the time away thinking my own thoughts about life and death and if the sermon went on too long, about important concerns, how many gophers were in my traps, whether we could play Run Sheep Run that evening. We retrieved the flowers after everyone had departed the church solemnly and in tears, and carried them to cars for the trip to the cemetery. Our final chore was to place them on the casket or arrange them around the grave and be quietly attentive for the rest of the final rites.

Especially I remember Mr. Vroman's funeral. In the church, I laid my bouquet down and then stood transfixed, staring at the effigy that laid there. That was not Mr. Vroman. Oh yes, it was as neat as he was, it even had the funny little goatee he had, but Mr. Vroman, small man that he was, moved with authority, commanded with a look. This—this thing was made of wax and it was a funny color and suddenly I began to cry. Not for Mr. Vroman, I am afraid, but for me. What could you trust if even Mr. Vroman wasn't real, if somehow they hid him and substituted this thing for him? Dying was a really terrible thing, I realized. It turned you into something else, something I didn't like. It made me think of the poor little birds I occasionally saw on the ground who seemed to kind of shrivel up in the dust. Or even worse, of the dead dog I saw one time that swelled in the summer heat. I made up my mind I would not die, would not, would not, no matter what they did to me to make me. And after that I kept my eyes averted when I laid my flowers down beside the coffin.

A young woman who had been our hired girl once briefly, died in childbirth. Dad and Mother looked very sad when they heard and tears rolled down his face. The funeral was held in the country and it was cold and there were a lot of people and they all cried and ate and blew their noses and the minister prayed for a very long time. The best part was when my father and three other men sang together, but even that was sad. She looked kind of pretty in her casket, but she didn't look real.

When my youngest brother was a baby he got sick and had convulsions, and the doctor came and the county nurse, Mrs. Hegel, and they made me go outside. I was afraid he would die and my mother was afraid too. I could tell because her face was so white and her lips got thin. He didn't die and in a few days he acted just like he did before he got sick. We were all glad, but my mother and father both looked young again and my mother smiled and my father whistled.

I was sick a lot in the winter time. When I had whooping cough, they put a bed for me in the dining room and my mother slept on a cot there so she could keep coal on the stove and keep the steam going. She would drape a sheet over my bed and make me breathe in the moisture. I can still see her thin white face hanging over me begging me to eat, "just a little honey, just a little." I tried because I didn't want to turn dead, and after a long time I got better.

There weren't very many medicines to cure things but tonics were supposed to help you endure and live through the sickness. There was castor oil and castoria which we seemed to have to take for every illness, a few white sugar pills and that was about it. Our good doctor introduced cod liver oil into our lives, but he shook it into some very tasty sweet red wine and we didn't mind it at all. I remember once when I was sick and white and skinny, he told my mother, "Just give her a chocolate bar now and then, a plain one, no nuts, let her have it when she wants it, it's good for her." I loved him for that. Some of my friends wore asafetida bags around their necks to ward off illness. Asafetida was an evil smelling herb and kids were known to take it off and hide it when out from under parental eyes. In some families kids had to take spring tonics of sulfur and molasses, maybe every morning for a week. Fortunately, our parents didn't believe in either of those remedies.

When the mother of some friends died, everyone felt very sad for them and my sister Kathleen and I went to their house where the casket was in the parlor. There was a picture of her in her casket in a sort of frame on top of it. Later that picture in that same frame hung in their parlor. I can still see her black hair and thin face with eyes closed, but I knew she wasn't asleep against the satin pillow with the ruffle. After that when we went there, I tried to stay in the kitchen.

I was afraid of death, but the cemetery was not a scary place for me. Sometimes we played there among the gravestones and on Decoration Day, the day we now call Memorial Day, we all stood around and sang and recited the poem about Flanders Field where poppies grow, and thought about the grave markers row on row. No one in our family died during that war, at least not our family in the United States. My grandmother had mourned because her sons went overseas to fight her sisters' and brothers' sons who stayed behind in Germany. I don't know if any of my mother's German cousins died, but they could have and it made my grandma sad. I realized dying was a very unhappy thing for everybody and I did not want to do it.

My father had some funny stories about death and dying he loved to tell. He told about Pat and Mike who were on their way to Kelly's funeral but they stopped off at every bar to bolster their courage. "Ah," says Pat, "sure dyin' is a terrible thing. I'll hate to see old Kelly like that." And they had a couple of drinks. Then Mike sighed, "Poor Kelly, a good soul he was and to end up like this," and they drank again. Finally having recited all of Kelly's good points and comforted themselves with many stops along the way, they staggered up the steps to Kelly's parlor and squinted at a row of burning candles. They dropped to their knees to offer a Hail Mary and Pat opened his eyes and gasped, "Ah poor Kelly, but what a set of teeth the man had," and the two of them collapsed in a heap against the piano.

My aunts told of going to a mortuary for the funeral of a young friend. They got lost and arrived late to hear the priest saying the final words about this wonderful God-lovin' woman who was forgiven her sins and was now happy in the arms of Christ. With the other mourners, sobbing at the early demise of their dear friend, they made their way to the casket, to see the raddled face of a perfect stranger with dyed red hair and a very large nose. Overcome with laughter, they covered their faces, pretending to be grief stricken to the point of hysterics, and rushed out to the street, but not before they heard someone say, "Ah the poor things, they must have been close."

I found death final and frightening in its reality, but also funny, and quite comfortable once there were only the symbols left to deal with, chunks of granite with names and dates, carvings of lilies and angels and a carpet of wildflowers in the spring. My friend Pauline and I used to dream about what it would be like when it was our turn. We drew pictures of our gravestones; they were always very large, with many kind words engraved upon them, and flowers. I thought I might like the figure of Jesus on mine, but I also favored St. Thomas Aquinas and a lamb, maybe both. Pauline fancied a weeping mother Mary. We never arrived at final decisions before something else came along and distracted our attention and we forgot about dying until it happened to someone we knew. And then we wished not to think about it in relation to ourselves—it was too real.

When I think of my grandfather's funeral, I think in snapshots; my memory is like an exhibit of these still photographs.

I see my grandparent's bedroom with all of us crowded in there together and the casket in front of us. The furniture has been moved out. There are my uncles, Albert, August, Edwin and Ernest. Not Calvin, he is dead. And my Aunt Martha, Uncle Ernest's wife and their two children, my cousins Buddy and Peggy. We are there, my father and mother, Kathleen and I. I don't remember my little brothers. My mother's much younger sister, Aunt Lisette is there, and I can't see them but I can't believe the Hilgemanns weren't there—Grandma's brother, I thought of him as "old Uncle Ernest" and Aunt Ella, my oldest cousin Gretchen, and probably the rest of the Hilgemann children.

In that picture my grandmother stood straight and still—totally still. Her broad forehead and her face looked carved from some kind of pale, slightly rough stone. Her hair was combed straight back as usual with just a hint of crimpy ridges from her curling iron in the sides, all of it neatly secured in a bun which she wore rather high above her neck. She wore her black silk Sunday dress and some kind of jewelry. I can't tell if it was gold and pearls or just gold—a pin I think.

I could just see the top of my grandfather's face in the casket—a long shiny box with lots of silver on it, up on a stand with wheels. There was white satin around him. It didn't really look like Grandpa, and yet it did. He was very pale, very quiet. I could see the beginning of his mustache and his hair, mostly still brown. I didn't want to look at him because he looked like what my daddy had told me he was, he looked dead. But I couldn't stop and it made me dizzy and my head hurt. I felt a terrible pain like a hand somewhere inside of me—kind of high, above my belly button. When it squeezed, all of me hurt, even my throat got tight and hard.

It was so quiet you could hear shoes creak and coat sleeves rub against one another. Outside the bedroom, in the parlor, were the rest of the mourners, and maybe some who were not sad, only curious. Uncle Henry, Grandpa's brother, must have been there, or maybe he was in with us, with his wife and family. I can't see that picture.

There were words spoken I'm sure, but I don't remember them. I think the squeaky organ in the parlor played a hymn or two, someone did, and people sang with lonesome, quivery voices. There were no tears. The faces around me were stern. I wondered if they all had hands squeezing inside of them.

Next we were in cars, Model Ts and touring cars, and then standing at the cemetery beside a hole in the ground, a big hole with dirt piled all around. We were all bundled against the wind, Grandma in her heavy coat. The uncles urged her to sit down, but she couldn't seem to bend at first. Finally she sat stiff on the edge of her chair like she didn't want to stay there. When the casket began to sink into the hole, the hand came again inside me. It squeezed until I couldn't breathe, my throat ached and tears made my eyes feel like bursting because they wanted to come but they couldn't.

That morning my father said, "You have to get dressed if you want to say good-bye to Grandpa." But I didn't want to say good-bye. I wanted Grandpa just the way he always was. You said good-bye and left and when you came back you said hello again. A last good-bye, Daddy had said. What a terrible, lonesome thing to say. Who would bring me lemon drops and cherries from downtown when I was visit-

ing? Who would take me riding in his Ford coupe out to
visit the farms around the town where he lived? And show
me where to hunt for eggs and how he milked the cow, and
squirt warm milk into my mouth, and let me crawl inside to
smell the smokehouse where he made ham and bacon? Who
would be there to listen to me talk stories and say my letters and eat milk toast with Grandma and me while we ate
supper? Later, in the back seat of our Model T, I told myself I didn't believe it, Grandpa wasn't dead. He'd be there
in his chair in the dining room. He'd call me *liebchen*.

I didn't say good-bye to Grandpa there by the hole in
the ground. I couldn't leave him in the cold and the dark—
if I didn't say good-bye, then he wouldn't be there. And
when we drove back to the house and everybody ate and
talked and told stories, I went outside and played with my
cousins and ran hard and yelled very loud so I wouldn't
think of him. And once, Grandma came out in the yard
with her arms wrapped around herself and stood there and
watched us, her face heavy and sad.

I had heard my mother and father talking that morning about how they had to have the funeral in my grandparents' house because Grandpa couldn't have a funeral
in the church. He hadn't been saved, the church people
said. He wasn't good enough. He was very, very good to me
but that wasn't what they meant.

The church that didn't want him was the only one in
town. I didn't like it. They said everything in German and
everyone was very stiff and their faces looked very hard.
The building looked hard too, small and square and plain,
nothing about it made you want to go in. And they talked
about hellfire and sin, the minister did, the pastor, and he
glared and shook his finger. I think he hated everyone, even
the ones who came to church, although how anyone could

hate Grandma I couldn't imagine. But my grandfather was a sinner who didn't go to church and he wouldn't ask the pastor or the church for forgiveness, he wouldn't say he was bad to them. I guess you could be a sinner if you were willing to say so out loud.

My grandmother tried to make up for Grandpa by giving money to the church and helping to keep it clean and in summer when the country kids came in for German catechism studies, they stayed at my grandparents' house and ate their meals there. She wanted my grandpa to be forgiven, especially when he got sick and had the operation at Mayo Brothers in Rochester, Minnesota, and she tried.

But it was a very strict church, very hard-hearted, I thought. Once my uncle and aunt and another couple were sitting around on a Saturday night drinking some home brew and playing cards, and they decided to go sledding. The women put on my uncle's overalls and old stocking caps and they took the children's sleds to the pasture outside of town and slid down the gentle hills. I'm sure they laughed a lot and threw snowballs and carried on in a way the church thought was undignified and downright sinful. And the next Sunday they were called by name before the congregation, humiliated and accused of all kinds of bad things. I was glad I didn't have to say good-bye to Grandpa in that place.

On our way home from the funeral with my parents, I thought about saying good-bye to Grandma, how her eyes had looked kind of milky and her silk dress had felt stiff and rustly, and how she smelled of talcum powder and soap and something else—a grandma smell. I wanted to say good-bye to Grandpa then too, but the hand came and squeezed inside me and made me feel sick it hurt so much.

I knew my father and mother weren't thinking about

us as we drove home. He stared at the road and she looked straight ahead, kind of angry. Daddy had said once that my mother couldn't forgive Grandpa because he was so strict and hard on his family, on her and her brothers and sister when they were young, and on Grandma, and he drank too much before he got his long sickness. I think she was glad he changed, but it hurt her to watch him be so different with his grandchildren. She remembered always being scared and worried when she was young and he was around. Now her face looked like Grandma's, hard and carved out of stone, and her eyes like she couldn't see. My father said Grandpa was the victim of his time and place and he asked Mother to try to forgive him.

I curled into my corner of the back seat and put my head way down inside my arms and then I cried. I think that meant good-bye, Grandpa.

Mother's Day and the Model T

⟋

IT WAS INTERESTING to watch the interaction between my parents. I realize now there was a constant game of one-upmanship going on between them—a need for each of them to prove something to the other. And I was never sure who would be the winner in these usually quiet struggles.

Their relationship didn't frighten me—I wasn't worried that they would part. Mother happily cooked Dad's favorite foods and served him the choice portions even when we had company and Dad was always thinking up surprises for Mother on special occasions. The things around our house that she treasured most were often presents from him—like the Chinese red bookcase one Christmas, her birthday pearls (not real ones, of course) and now the biggest gift of all, a car, our first, for Mother's Day. I did notice that Mother smiled a rather peculiar smile when Dad announced that the car would be coming in time for her special day. He had been pushing hard for the purchase and Mother had been resisting, worrying about whether they could possibly afford it and still keep us all in shoes.

Behind our house, near the lot line was a doorless unpainted building, once probably a wagon or buggy shed. We used it to house our coal supply and the kind of litter that is usually found in attic and cellar, neither of which we had.

When we got the car, the coal had to move over and share space with the Model T. I remember as if it were yesterday that May Saturday it came, a shiny, black, high-topped wonder that was to open up for us the pleasures of Sunday drives, visits to the farmhouses of friends, a trip to the Black Hills and the delights of picnics by the river. Koch, his whole name was Garrett Koch, pronounced Cook, who owned the local garage, delivered the Model T to our house and demonstrated its workings to my father and then, surprised perhaps, but amiable, to my mother. It was her present, she announced, and she would be a driver.

My sister and I and our little brother stood at a respectful distance and listened to Koch's instructions to "Advance the spark now—clutch it, clutch it Denny," and Whoa, man, whoa." Mother picked up the knack of the thing a bit more quickly than Dad and first thing we knew one at a time they were whirling out onto the road and sailing off in sprays of gravel, little stones spitting from beneath the skinny tires.

Noon dinner was very late that day and by the time our parents felt secure enough in driving skills to offer rides to their children, we were more interested in the beef stew that was cooking on the coal stove, and we feared, beginning to smell a little scorched. Mother agreed that we should eat now and ride later and herded us toward the wash basin.

We dipped our hands into the basin of tepid water and dunked our little brother's, wiped on the skinny cotton towel that hung on a nail and tumbled into the kitchen. Mother was dishing up bowls of stew and pouring milk from the glass jar that Dad pulled up from the well in a galvanized pail that served us as ice box.

Savoring thick slices of crusty bread and gravy, we listened with growing excitement to Dad's plan for the rest of the day. "Why don't we drive up to Artas and see your folks, Minnie? We could stop by the Hofers and say hello."

"Oh, Den, it's too late. We'd have to spend the night."

"Why not, Min? They'd welcome us and you could spend Mother's Day with your mother."

Artas was twenty-seven miles away over dusty gravel roads, and to get to the Hofers' you had to ford a stream in a couple of places—not a journey you undertook lightly past the middle of the day, especially with three kids (my youngest brother was still "on the way") who had to have feet and faces washed and clean clothes on before you could start. But Dad won the argument as he usually did with enthusiastic support from us, and Mother called her mother to warn of our coming. The thought of the ride in the new car and the chance to see the Hofers and Grandma and our cousins in Artas was enthralling.

Buster had to be fed and brushed so he could share the ride. Dad arranged for someone to ring the church bell for him on Sunday morning.

Finally, all of us washed and brushed, at least where it showed, Mother in her pretty voile dress and Dad in a clean white shirt, we were ready to set off. When Dad climbed into the driver's seat without even a questioning glance at Mother, she accepted the precedent with nothing more than a slight tightening of her jaw and a clearing of her throat. The three of us and Buster piled into the back seat and tumbled among ourselves as Dad fussed with starter and spark and finally climbed out glumly to crank, shouting unintelligible instructions to Mother about what to do inside the car. The engine finally caught, and Dad flung himself into the car and started backing toward the road and the ditch that ran in front of the house.

"Den-Den, watch . . .," Mother's voice faded, Dad braked, the motor died and we sat in a cloud of dust, braced for the wrath we knew would follow. Our father was a man of many talents, he could sing like a bird, tell a story that kept a roomful of people quiet, poetize and speechify, but he was no more a mechanic than a mouse. And his failures made him furious.

We could see Mother swallow the sharp words she wanted to say and make an effort to calm him down. She was sure that if he would just get out and change places, she could get the car started and smoothly on its way in no time, but she was wise enough not to say so. We huddled silently in the back seat until somebody's cat strolled into our yard and settled in the sun on the back stoop. Buster, a collie shepherd mix with long white and gold hair, liked that cat just fine, usually they tolerated each other without trouble, even sharing the same sunny spot now and then. But this was a different matter. She was settling in like an owner, and he was surrounded by glass and metal, helpless to establish his prior rights. Bedlam ensued. Buster whined and barked and waved his plumy tail in our faces. Kathleen and I grabbed him to shush him. We recognized the tension in the car and knew enough not to add to it. But by this time Jack, who was about eighteen months old, was tired of being cooped up, and when the dog accidentally struck him in the face with his hind feet, he began to howl. That was his modus-operandi, he didn't cry often but when he bothered, he bawled lustily. He started pounding on the window and the car rang and shook with all our efforts. Dad banged open the car door and climbed out yelling, "Everybody out, out, out, out now!"

We managed to untangle ourselves. Buster claimed the stoop; Mother wearily climbed out and shooed us into the shade while she dealt with Dad. Within minutes he had had a cool drink at the pump, and for once we were smart enough not to insist upon equal treatment. He and the car had cooled down and apparently decided to settle their differences. We all packed in once again, and Dad backed out and around until he could drive out frontwards and miss the ditch. We were off to Grandma's house for Mother's Day.

The thrill of the ride wore off more than a bit as the dust flew up from our wheels almost obscuring any view, and we faced a choice of sweltering and easier breathing with the windows up or inhaling thick, dry gulps of what passed for air. Buster settled peacefully on the floor, Jack went to sleep across our laps, and Mother and Dad rode in what seemed to us to be tense silence. My sister and I listened and watched for signs of peace.

Finally Dad chuckled and said, "Did you ever hear the one about 'the frog that went a courtin'?" and began to sing verse after verse of the silly song about the frog and Miss Mousy and their possible wedding until we were giggling and laughing and trying to join in the chorus. Even Mother unbent and smiled and gave him a light slap on the shoulder and said, "Oh, Den, you are too much."

That was the first of many journeys in the Model T.

Mother was pregnant, although I didn't know it at the time, and she was ready to get a hired girl to help with things these last months and be there to take over when the baby came. Mother at the wheel, my little brother Jack, close to two, and I, going on five, in the back seat of the Model T, were on our way to get the "country girl" who would be helping us, Mother hoped.

It was a clear pleasant day, neither hot nor cold, and we rolled along the narrow gravel road, crowned so that water would run off into the ditch when it rained. Per instruction, I was trying to keep my feisty toddler brother from climbing out the window or eating crumbs from the last picnic off the car floor. Probably I grabbed a little too fast, pressed a little too hard, for he let out a yelp and Mother turned to see what the problem was. The wheels veered too close to the road edge, and we slipped sideways and tipped over into the ditch, quite gently, not even a window broke.

As soon as she realized that Jack and I weren't hurt, "Get him out of the tool box, Elizabeth," Mother said, and I did. He was standing on his head among the wrenches and pliers and the motor crank, but except for a bit of oil showing through his light brown hair, he was unmarked and thankfully silent, too surprised to cry. Mother climbed out of the door and slid to the ground and took the baby I pushed up until he dangled in mid-air, and then I got out too. With the two of us safely shooed across the ditch, Mother began to examine the new car for damage. Color came back into her face when she realized the catastrophe was far from total and she lifted Jack and held my chin in her other hand.

"Elizabeth, you have to be a big girl and get help. The next car that comes, we'll get you a ride back to town and you go to the office and get your father. Tell him to come and bring Koch to get us out of here."

Minutes later, a truck loomed high and white, its metal tank shimmering in the sun, throwing up dust as it headed toward us and town. Mother stepped to the side of the road carrying Jack and, still gripping my hand, she managed to wave.

"Why, sure, Mrs. Mills, I know Mr. Mills, sure, I'll take her there and don't you worry, I'll come back with 'em and help get you out of there and right side up if they need me. Now you're not hurt, are you, little lady, or this peanut here?" He patted Jack, who looked at him doubtfully.

With a boost from the grinning driver, I clambered way up into the truck seat, waved to Mother and twisted around to see her anxious face watch us out of sight. The ride was short and noisy, with little conversation. How strange the world looked from way up in the air, I would see everything, even, I was sure, the wiggle path that a snake must have made in the dust, and how the wheat growing next to the road hung its heavy heads, ready to be harvested.

It seemed no time before we were in front of my father's office. My new friend went in with me to tell him what happened and then drove us both down the street to Koch's garage. My father thanked the driver and invited him to dinner next time he came to town. The rescue truck headed back toward Mother and Jack, with Daddy and me in the seat beside Mr. Koch.

Without even the use of the tackle and crane on the back of the truck, they lifted the car and set it on its wheels. Koch waved us off, and Dad drove home, smiling just a little. The car had suffered barely a scratch, but the question of who was the better driver had taken a turn in his favor. Mother rode in relieved silence. The hired girl would have to wait.

For longer trips the car was equipped with something called a carrier bolted to the passenger side fender. This fold-up accordion-like guard was crammed with the necessary changes of clothes, food, extra bedding, toys and sometimes a tent and camp stove. Inside the car was usually more food, water, a damp towel to keep us from sticking to one another or the leather seat permanently, the absolutely necessary pee jar, our parents, the dog and after Bob was born, four kids playing, fighting, sleeping, passing the time until we got wherever we were going.

The trips in that car were a perfect metaphor for life in our family—tension, forbearance, laughter, Mother smoothing the way, Dad entertaining, we kids fitting in the best we could.

Widow's Walk

~

F OR SOME REASON my grandparents' house always made
me think of a ship. Probably it was because of the
widow's walk outside the upstairs bedroom, a special little
railed porch that allowed you to look out over the small
cluster of houses and trees that was Artas. How it came to
be built in a South Dakota town as far from the ocean as
you could get, no one ever explained to me.

From its vantage point you could see the railroad tracks
stretching out into the prairie, the cemetery, the creek, the
gravel pit and the Dutch Reform Church and Jarhouse's
store. It seemed to me it was always quiet there, only the
sound of an occasional train whistle, a horse and wagon
passing, or a Ford crunching the gravel broke the quiet.
People walked somberly, and spoke German to one another
in low voices. There was very little color, white houses with
a bit of green trim perhaps, neat gardens devoted to potatoes and beans and corn with only an occasional patch of
mignonette or a few hollyhocks.

My grandmother cherished the plum tree in their front yard and the chamomile that grew on the ground around it. We children loved to gather cocoons from under the rails of the fence that separated the house from the barn and smokehouse. We would crawl carefully to the roof of a shed and put them on the ridge where the sun would bring them to hatch and then follow their dancing flight until dusk fell and they were replaced in our attention by fireflies.

I loved going to my grandparents' house. It was a treat for a middle child to be for a little while, a doted-upon only. I relished being given all the attention I wanted and yet having the freedom I was used to, to roam the town, visit the friends I had made, swim in the creek. When Grandpa was well enough we would drive to the country or walk to the store together and sometimes I liked to just sit quietly with Grandma.

Her hands were rough and large knuckled. I can see them now pulling the feathers from a chicken, then she singed it over the open burner of the coal range and slit its abdomen to salvage the heart, liver and gizzard and dumped the rest of the insides into the slop pail. She held the bloody bird carefully over the pail to keep her apron clean. The cuffs were turned back and pushed above her elbows to protect her long sleeves. Her dress was always dark, gray or brown probably, sometimes with a tiny figure of another dull color and over it she wore a dark gray apron.

One afternoon we sat together companionably, Grandma explaining each stage of the preparations for supper in her heavy German accent, warning me to be careful of the *schmear*, the mess. The click and squeak of the gate in the white picket fence and the sound of heavy feet on the wooden walkway alerted us to the imminence of company. Quickly Grandma dropped the bird into a pail of clean water beside her, then shook it and rolled it in a clean towel. She pulled down her sleeves, unrolled the cuffs and whisked off the used apron in one practiced motion. As she opened the kitchen door she was tying on a clean white apron and tucking a stray hair under her hairnet.

The guests stood on the kitchen stoop, their heads covered with dark cloths, wearing heavy, long sleeved dresses and aprons, one quite indistinguishable from another. They entered, gray eminences, and seated themselves around the table while my grandmother shook down the coal range, set the coffee to heat, and brought out a plate of *kuchen*. I could understand just enough of the German to know that my presence, my height, weight, my overalls, my resemblance to my mother and my father's Irish impecuniousness were being commented upon. "Ach, such a *kleine* man, *und* a *lehrer* yet, no *grundstuck*, not even a *kuh*," they mourned. A teacher with neither property or livestock was of little use in their eyes, certainly not as a son-in-law.

The old women made inquiries after my grandfather's health, accompanied by gloomy headshakes and soft moans. "Yah, yah," they mourned, bodies swaying. They were already enjoying his funeral although he would live for almost another year. No matter the subject, every comment, every question was accompanied by mournful sighs and "Ach yah—sooo." Smiles appeared to me to be mere grimaces.

"So, chicken, (shicken they pronounced it or *huhn*) for the supper, yah?" somehow managed to be a grieved accusation. Their lives were one long lamentation. Finally they finished their coffee, pinched up the last crumb of *kuchen* and stood to go. Back to their own kitchens to plunge their red arms into pails of hot water and slit their own chickens' gizzards.

When the door shut and we heard the gate squeal good-bye, my grandmother laid her hand on my head for a moment before she whisked off the clean apron, "So," she said, "the blackbirds are gone again."

In the years that followed my grandfather's death, my grandmother spent more and more time with us. Hers was a double life. Later when she came to our house in Pierre, her trunk which sat in the attic the rest of the time, was brought down and she opened it. For summer, out came pretty, short sleeved voiles and cottons, blue and white prints, soft yellow, mint green. With them were dainty colored aprons and white shoes. For winter there were rich wine red and forest green or black silk with colored figures. There was a little tray of gold chains and a gem studded bird brooch to wear with them.

For the weeks she stayed with us, my grandmother hummed a lot or sang softly under her breath, old German songs. She laughed, a bit reluctantly at first, but finally freely at my father's Irish stories. "Ach you, Denny," she would say shaking her head. She was always available to comfort a sad child or rock a sick one and pass out slices of jelly bread or sugar bread.

Each time, the day before she left again for Artas, the trunk would be packed away and she put on her second best black silk for traveling. It always seemed to me that something more happened to her; it was as if she faded a little before my eyes. Her rich voice with its heavy German accent became reedy and a gray cloud seemed to follow her. Some of my tears at our partings were because I would miss her, some because I sensed a small death to mourn.

The Last Day

ᲢᲘ

I T WAS MY LAST DAY. I woke to a dark room. The only light
was little strips at the sides of the shades that didn't quite
cover the windows. I remembered my parents pulling them
tight when we went to bed last night. "Sleep tight," they
had said. "Tomorrow is a busy day but you don't have to be
up so early."

There was no usual clatter of dishes, no comforting
smell of coffee and burning toast downstairs. My parents
were talking in muffled tones and quietly moving things.
Occasionally I could hear the rattle of paper, the swish of
boxes being shoved around.

I swallowed hard trying to get rid of the feelings that
were coming back. I remembered now crying last night,
stuffing the covers in my mouth so no one would hear. I
wanted to cry again but I knew it was no use. It wouldn't
change anything. I lay in my warm bed, my back to the
window. I would think of something, anything that would
blot out the day ahead—something ordinary, not too happy,

not sad, just plain everyday. But nothing was ordinary. Everything hurt.

I reached out my hand to touch the pile of clothes on the chair by my side of the bed. My overalls, my plaid shirt—a boy's shirt I loved. I wasn't dressing for school. My sister breathed deeply for a moment and turned toward me. I knew I shouldn't wake her. I slid out of bed, grabbed the clothes and my shoes from under the bed and tiptoed down the stairs.

Mother and Dad glanced at me abstractly. I was just another problem, a logistics problem to be solved. There was no fire in the coal stove, no cream of wheat bubbling, no coffee perking. And suddenly I was desperately hungry. If only by some magic my usual breakfast appeared, I would eat it all, the last crumb of toast, no complaints about it being too brown, too crisp. I would not play in my cream of wheat or dribble brown spots on the tablecloth trying to skim the skin off my cocoa and put it on my plate.

I sidled into the front room and put on my clothes. Mother bustled in with an armload of table linen to go in a box. I said I was going outside and she barely glanced my way. "Don't go far, we're going across the road for breakfast, you know."

I knew. Garrett Koch was driving one car to our new home with part of the family and some of our stuff and Dad would drive ours. A truck would bring the rest. Mrs. Koch, Mae, was giving us breakfast

Outside the sun was coming up bright and big, little frost flowers were melting off the weeds and the back steps. The vacant lot next door glittered with sun on the rime covered thistles and spider webs sparkled like diamonds. Smoke streamed out of chimneys, Buster came back into the yard after his morning stroll about town. We stood together and watched the mail truck stop in front of the post office, Allen's cat nosed through the weeds looking for an unwary breakfast. Everything was the same. But different. It wasn't mine anymore. We were moving to Pierre. Daddy had a new job, a good one.

"You'll love it," Dad said. "It has a library and the capitol buildings and movies."

"Electric lights," Mother said. "And indoor toilets and a furnace." You could tell Mother was excited. She wanted me to be excited too.

I could see the kids starting up the hill toward school. The Kightlinger kids, my friends Willis Kolodzie and Buddy, Albert Orth and there was Pauline and Erna. I stood in the shadow of the coal shed. They didn't see me or if they did, I was just as much a stranger to them as they were to me.

I walked around the church and peeked in the basement windows and lifted the lid of the badger box. I went in the outhouse and pulled my overalls down and sat on my hole, the left one. I never sat on the right one. I didn't like it. I didn't know why. A fly or two, slowed by the morning chill, last of the season, bumbled lazily in the little window above me. I hadn't bothered to shut the door tight, and Allen's cat poked an inquisitive nose in and backed out. It would be nice having a flush toilet, I guessed, and a real bathtub not just a tin wash tub. Sure, that would be good.

I wandered over to the coal shed again. Back of it is where we dug to China last summer,. although of course we didn't get to China. But we got deep, lots deeper than the graves they dug for dead people at the cemetery. We had had to put the dirt back when the first frost came and the ground was still bumpy. It was fun that summer sitting in the shade of the deep hole eating our jelly sandwiches and drinking lemonade.

Hans Anderson's house stared at me from behind the bushes that grew around it. It was a nice gray house and very neat. They didn't have any kids to dig holes and thrash through their garden.

The school bell rang—first call. I slumped down on the ground. It wasn't for me. I couldn't go. My heart tightened and shrunk until it was a hard little nut inside me. I'd never go to school there again, never double pump standing up on the swing with Sonny Larsen until we could see the roofs of the houses around. Never play knife, we didn't call it mumbledy peg—at recess or practice the broad jump for Rally Day or play Fox and Geese in the new snow. Pauline and I would never gather kids together and play school in our kitchen or in the shade of the house on a hot summer day.

I could taste the wild onions I would never pick again and see Miss Dynan's face smile at me when I spelled a hard word. Would my new school have a sand table and a Latta book and maps that pulled down so you could see where Grandma came from and where those people lived who wore rings around their necks to make them longer and things in their lips to make them big? Would a new teacher play the Victrola and let us put our heads on the desk and listen for the sounds in the music, like water rushing and happy people and horses clattering?

We went to breakfast at Koch's house and Mae gave us cinnamon rolls and bacon. It was good. And then Daddy said, "Come on now, Elizabeth, Kathleen, let's go up to school and you can say good-bye and then we have to go." Kathleen didn't want to go, she had said her good-byes and she was ready for the new world.

We walked to the school and Daddy held my hand. When we opened the door, I could smell it just like always,

kids, and wool, and breakfast, and chalk in the air. Everybody stared at me, and Miss Dynan made a little speech
and then she hugged me and I started to cry and Willis
cried and Pauline and even Benny.

That was my last day in Mound City. I rode in the back
seat with Buster and Bobby. Kathleen sat with Daddy.
Mother and Jack rode with Koch. All the way to Pierre,
Buster's big tail waved in my face and Bobby bounced up
and down most of the time. Daddy sang but I didn't.

Epilogue: Plain Art

H OW COULD I have been so enamored, in love actually, with such a plain, unembellished little town as Mound City, South Dakota? It sat there on the prairie, dusty and almost treeless, far from the river, surrounded by wheat fields and corn, barley and rye, the prairie wind nosing around its corners. I ask myself that question often and others ask me too. My sister, for example, who was enough older than I so that long before we left when she was twelve and I was nine, she had discovered all of its deficiencies. And she and I, close as we are now, two old ladies who chat on the telephone every weekend, were, still are, very different people. We need different things in our lives, admire one thing more than another, each of us. Whatever the reason, Mound City gave me something, a wonderful thing that has stayed with me, sustained me through this long life and helped me, I think, see the beauty in other places where I have found myself over the years.

Plain is the most descriptive word I can think of to

219 / Epilogue: Plain Art

describe that town, the people and the lives we led. Luxury, ease, would have been considered sin and sloth by many who lived there. It was, I think, in the character of prairie people then to admire things undecorated, or at least not overdecorated. So much of everyone's energy was required just to live, to stay warm in winter and decently fed and clothed. It is no wonder there was great aesthetic appreciation for a line of laundry sparkling in the sun publishing the housewife's talent. And the same appreciation was accorded shelves of preserves and jelly and jam.

My father hated the labor of it but took pleasure in a healthy potato patch and rows of green beans. Each autumn he nervously climbed the high ladder and removed the screens and mounted the storm windows on our two story house. And each spring he reversed the process. His pleasure was greater than just a job well done—it was an early victory over the elements and that fight went on eternally regardless of season. He could regard his handiwork with the eye of an artist.

I can see him on a sunny Saturday, wearing the most disreputable garments he owned, pressed twill trousers and a white shirt even my mother could not turn the collar of again or mend sufficiently for work day wear, shoveling a pungent mixture of dirt and manure around the perimeter of our house to keep out winter's icy breath. The only job I can think of that he would have disliked more was slaughtering a chicken for our Sunday dinner. That made him sick.

The "stupid bird" always got away from him once it was beheaded and flopped around the yard spraying blood for a minute before it fell dead. You could see his jaw tighten and his eyes tear. Those black eyebrow arches of his that we learned early to watch as predictors of his personal weather would be almost touching his hairline. When his eyebrows started to rise, you knew you were in for it and looked for a harbor safe from the storm. Mother was more practical. She felt for all live things too, but when the question "What's for dinner " came, she needed a good answer. So she plucked that chicken and eviscerated it with no show of emotion, conscience free I am sure. It was all part of taking care of her family.

When Sunday dinner appeared on the table, no one spared even a moment to mourn the poor bird. From Dad with his giant's share of breast meat right down to Bobby, the baby, gnawing on a drumstick, we devoured the good greasy brown skin and meat and the almost salty gravy and mashed potatoes with total relish. Fresh from the garden or canned, the green beans were dressed with diced bacon and vinegar stirred into the drippings. If the menu called for peas, they were liberally doused in cream and butter, and salted to our taste. Even in summer, salad as I think of it today didn't appear on our table. But the hot bacon fat and vinegar did its delicious trick wilting the garden lettuce and spiced up winter's thinly sliced cabbage.

Every meal had its share of pickles, and homemade bread was always accompanied by a jar or two of Mother's jam or jelly, chokecherry, grape, buffalo berry and the deep brown spicy applebutter that I loved.

We never skipped dessert. Mother turned out a succession of pies and cakes, cobblers, cookies, gingerbread and applesauce, suet puddings, chocolate, lemon, coconut and tapioca puddings too. Only on wash day and during the storms of housecleaning each spring and fall, were we reduced to a dish of sauce and a gingersnap to finish up a meal.

That tasty colorful variety of food, much of which came

from our own garden and all from my mother's magic touch with spices and sugar and vinegar, was an art exhibit in its own right. But of course we were not without our more conventional pursuits of the arts either. The old wooden Victrola, so tall I had to stand on a chair to wind it and set the needle on the big black disc, brought us opera arias with Galli-Curci and a man's tenor voice that I cannot attribute, John McCormack perhaps.

We washed and wiped the dishes to the strains of *An English Country Garden* or *Barcarole*. And often we listened to the recording of the *Two Black Crows* who reduced my sister and me to fits of laughter even when we had heard the record so many times we mouthed the lines with them, even before them. "If I get there first, I'll draw a line—if you get there first, you rub it out."

In school we were offered something called Music Appreciation when we were told to bow our heads, even allowed to lay them on the desk while we listened to scratchy recordings of famous orchestras playing important music. Music far above *Believe Me If All Those Endearing Young Charms,* which we often sang on Friday mornings, even more illustrious than *Santa Lucia* which I thought was the best. We were encouraged to listen for the signs of spring or of tragedy or sunshine that the music would reveal to us. My hand always waved first, I am afraid, for I was anxious to tell the teacher I had heard whatever was expected.

We also had a time every week for Art Appreciation when we all peered closely at famous paintings, reproductions of course, until every last child in the room, first through fourth grades, could identify "Boy With the Torn Hat" and "Blue Boy" and their painters and we all agreed Rosa Bonheur's horses were our favorite. These and many other prints were displayed around the walls of our schoolroom along with the ubiquitous portrait of George Washington, the American flag, and examples of our own finest efforts at drawing, penmanship and poetry.

Prairie mothers and fathers wanted the best for their children and did their best to give it to them, but their greatest admiration went to those things that helped carve a living out of the vast rolling landscape and impress upon it some order. If one did not do that, it was too big, too overwhelming, like living in the middle of the ocean with nothing but the ever distant horizon to stop the eye. It was each family's efforts to tame the prairie, to carve out a place and mark it, to make it our place, our home, that was the real artistry.